"Meet me tonight, Maggie,"

Jake said.

It was tempting. So tempting.

"Say yes."

Jake's tone was more of an order than a request, and years of hearing orders put her back up. She hated being pressured, especially by a man. She was supposed to be calling her own shots. Unfortunately, what she wanted was a little too close to what he wanted for her to get really angry.

"Just tonight?" she asked finally.

Jake paused a long moment. "I can't answer that question."

"Then I can't meet you tonight."

Jake shook his head, frustration warring with understanding. Finally he smiled. "What about tomorrow?"

Dear Reader,

March comes in like a lion with our latest FABULOUS FATHERS title, *Caleb's Son* by Laurie Paige. For Caleb Remmick, life was all work and no play. Until a woman from his past—and his adorable young son—forced Caleb to make room for love.

Anne Peters weaves a tale of love and betrayal in *His Only Deception.* Laura Erickson thought she had it all when a transfer overseas brought her into the arms of her handsome boss, Jonathan Devlin. But Jonathan had other reasons for wanting Laura by his side....

Don't miss *The Marriage Scheme*—Carla Cassidy's heartwarming story of two matchmaking teenagers who plot to get their parents together.

Also this month, find out why a woman can't resist *The Cowboy's Proposal* in this sexy new book from Dorsey Kelley. In Kristina Logan's *A Man Like Jake,* a handsome wanderer falls in love—*and* finds a home. And Donna Clayton rounds out the month with an emotional story of a jilted groom and the woman who longs to mend his broken heart in *Return of the Runaway Bride.*

Join us in the months to come for more books from some of your favorite authors, such as Diana Palmer, Debbie Macomber and Elizabeth August.

Until then, happy reading!

Anne Canadeo
Senior Editor

Please address questions and book requests to:
Reader Service
U.S.: P.O. Box 1325, Buffalo, NY 14269
Canadian: P.O. Box 1050, Niagara Falls, Ont. L2E 7G7

A MAN LIKE JAKE
Kristina Logan

Silhouette
ROMANCE™
Published by Silhouette Books
America's Publisher of Contemporary Romance

To Barbara, Karen and Melissa—
you're the best!

 SILHOUETTE BOOKS

ISBN 0-373-08998-8

A MAN LIKE JAKE

Copyright © 1994 by Barbara Beharry Freethy

This edition published by arrangement with Harlequin Enterprises B.V.

® and TM are trademarks of Harlequin Enterprises B.V., used under license. Trademarks indicated with ® are registered in the United States Patent and Trademark Office, the Canadian Trade Marks Office and in other countries.

Printed in U.S.A.

KRISTINA LOGAN

is a native Californian and a former public-relations professional who spent several exciting years working with a variety of companies whose business interests ranged from wedding consulting to professional tennis, high technology and the film industry. Now the mother of two small children, she divides her time between her family and her first love, writing.

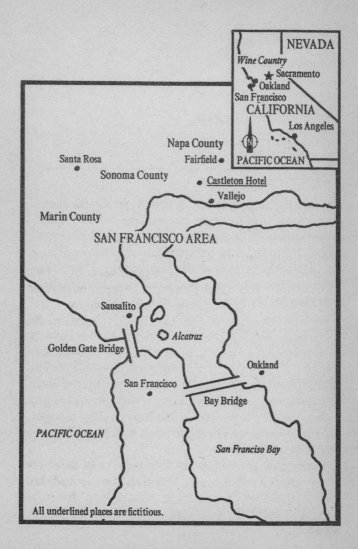

NEVADA

Wine Country

★ Sacramento

Oakland

San Francisco

CALIFORNIA

Los Angeles

PACIFIC OCEAN

N

Santa Rosa

Napa County

Fairfield

Sonoma County

Castleton Hotel

Vallejo

Marin County

SAN FRANCISCO AREA

Sausalito

Alcatraz

Golden Gate Bridge

Oakland

San Francisco

Bay Bridge

PACIFIC OCEAN

San Franciso Bay

All underlined places are fictitious.

Chapter One

He was the kind of man her father would have shot on sight—dark curly hair that drifted past the collar of his black leather jacket, a day's growth of beard on his face and a small gold earring looped through one ear.

Maggie Gordon smiled to herself as she watched the man walk the length of the luxurious lobby. He knew he was being watched. He'd probably known it since he'd roared up in front of the prestigious Castleton Hotel on his motorcycle and casually deposited it with the valet. And judging by the swagger of his walk, he didn't give a damn what the people of the Napa Valley thought, especially those conservative souls watching his progress through the lobby.

Lucky guy, not to have to follow the rules or worry about what others thought. Maggie had never had that kind of freedom, not with a marine colonel for a father, and certainly not with a rigid boss like Harry Stone.

The thought of her manager made her stand up straighter, and the grin that was lurking at the corners of her mouth vanished. Her shoulders stiffened and she forced her lips into a cool smile, donning the professional demeanor of a proper Castleton employee. With two weeks left on her probation period, she could not afford to mess up—not with three payments left to make the down payment on the house she was currently renting.

The man's booted heels clicked against the marble floor as he came to a halt in front of the desk. He set his black duffel bag down on the floor, casting one sweeping look around the lobby as he did so, obviously amused by the attention he was drawing. Then he directed his gaze at her, his bright green eyes sparkling with mischief.

It was difficult not to respond to such an engaging look, but somehow she managed. "May I help you?" Maggie asked, pleased by the cool tone of her voice. She would not let his rebellious charm get to her, even if it did strike a chord of understanding deep within her.

The man stared at her long and hard. Finally, he spoke, but his words came as a complete surprise. "Kathy?" His loud voice rang through the lobby, and Maggie looked at him in astonishment.

"What?"

"I've missed you, darling. Come here and give me a kiss."

"My name isn't Kathy—"

He cut her off as he reached across the counter and grabbed her shoulders. He didn't give her time to do anything but open her mouth, which was a definite mistake. His kiss was hot and hungry, his lips moving against hers in a sensuous manner that was unlike anything she had felt before. He tasted like beer and popcorn, and the heat from his body rushed over her like a warm summer breeze. It was a teasing, tantalizing kiss, and she let it go on far too long.

"Miss Gordon!" Harry Stone's shocked voice brought her to her senses. Maggie immediately pulled away. "What is going on here?" he demanded, his homely, round face turning red with anger.

Maggie's hand flew to her mouth, her lips still tingling from the impact of his kiss. "I—I—" She looked at her boss in confusion and then back at the man who had started it all.

He was grinning without a trace of remorse in his eyes. Instead, there was a sparkle and the lingering gleam of passion, which only made her feel more unsettled. It was time to regain control of the situation. "Why did you do that?" she demanded.

"I thought you wanted me to." He folded his arms on the countertop and smiled at her.

"I did not. I didn't give you any encouragement. And you called me Kathy."

He straightened up and gave her a look of complete innocence. "You mean you're not Kathy?"

"No, I'm not."

"Do you know this man?" Harry interrupted, eyeing them both with displeasure.

"No. He mistook me for someone else, didn't you?"

The man tipped his head, sending her a long, lingering look. He reached out a hand and tucked a stray hair behind her ear. "I guess you don't look much like her, after all, and you sure as hell don't kiss like her."

Maggie took a step back and swallowed hard. It was crazy to feel such a strong reaction to a simple touch of a hand on her hair. "You owe me an apology."

He shrugged. "But I can't say I'm sorry. It wouldn't be the truth."

"Do you have a reservation?" Harry interrupted again. "If not, I'm afraid . . ."

"The name is Hollister."

"I don't recall that name being booked," Harry replied.

"Why don't you check? You might be surprised."

Maggie typed out his name on the computer and waited. "J. Hollister?"

"That's right. My friends call me Jake."

She ignored that leading piece of information. "How do you want to pay for this?"

He slipped out a credit card and pushed it across the counter. "Plastic, of course."

Maggie ran the card through the machine for authorization and then completed the transaction while Harry Stone watched over her shoulder.

"Room 316 would be a better choice," Harry said as the assigned room number appeared on the monitor screen.

She cast him a quick look. Room 316 was on the street side and over the garbage can pickup. "We have an opening on the fourth floor," she replied in a hushed voice.

"No, that one is reserved." He reached over her and punched the buttons to change the room number. Maggie had no choice but to hand Mr. Hollister a key and hope he wouldn't come to her to complain.

Jake sent her a thoughtful glance and then signed the credit card receipt without comment.

"Enjoy your stay," Maggie said politely, adding silently that she hoped it would be shorter than the ten days he had registered for.

"At least it's off to a good start," he said wryly.

Jake picked up his duffel bag and swung it over one shoulder. Then he sauntered toward the elevator, his long, lean legs encased in a pair of tight, worn blue jeans that had a very nice fit. Maggie took in a deep breath and let it out slowly, willing herself to look away, but he was by far the sexiest man she had seen in a long time. And that kiss... Her heart was still pounding against her ribs, her pulse racing faster than it did during aerobics. What on earth was the matter with her? You'd think she'd never seen a man before.

Finally, the elevator doors opened, and Jake stepped inside. It wasn't until the doors closed shut that Maggie turned away.

"Your behavior was abominable," Harry said immediately.

"Mr. Stone, please. I do *not* know why that man kissed me. I did nothing to encourage him."

He looked at her in obvious disbelief. "Really? I've been working in the hotel business for over fifteen years, and I've never seen that happen before."

"I guess there's a first for everything."

"Your flippancy is not appreciated. I'm putting this on your report, Miss Gordon. Any more incidents like this, and you may want to think about looking for another job."

"No. I love this job. I need it." It went against the grain to beg, but for that tiny cottage on the edge of the woods, she would do just about anything.

"Then do it, quietly and efficiently. This is a luxury hotel. We are courteous, helpful and above all discreet. We do not cause scenes, nor do we engage in illicit activity at the front desk."

"Yes, sir. I mean, no, sir. We don't cause scenes—sir," she added for extra emphasis.

Harry sighed. "I have to go out for an hour. Try not to get into any more trouble before dinner."

Maggie nodded, breathing a sigh of relief as her manager left the reception area. She just wanted to get back to work and forget about her encounter with Jake Hollister.

"You certainly do liven this place up." Karen Monte, a tall, slim blonde, walked around the counter and slipped her purse into a desk drawer.

Maggie gave her a wry smile. "What did you see?"

"Everything. I was just coming back from my break when I saw you kissing a very interesting-looking guy."

"*He* was kissing *me*. In fact, he just reached over and grabbed me. It was the strangest thing. He said he thought I was someone else."

Karen shook her head in amazement. "Why don't things like that ever happen to me? The most attention I got was when a foreign tour group asked me to be in their holiday photograph." She paused, taking a quick glance around the lobby, but most of the interested onlookers were now going about their own business. "So, how was it?"

"How was it?" Maggie echoed. "It was—" She shrugged her shoulders, trying to think of an adequate description, like *wonderful* or *fantastic* or *unbelievable*. No, those words weren't right at all. She threw up her hands in disgust. "It was terrible. He almost got me fired."

"But how was it?" Karen persisted. "You didn't exactly slap his face."

Maggie shifted her feet uncomfortably, dropping her gaze to the computer keyboard. "I don't know. Not bad, I guess.'' She looked up and smiled at Karen's doubtful look. "Okay, it was pretty good, if you like that macho stuff.''

"And you don't?''

"No. If he hadn't taken me completely by surprise, I would have slapped his face or kicked him you-know-where.''

"Ouch.'' Karen laughed. "When I saw Mr. Stone, I decided it would be better for me to wait until you were through.''

"Chicken.''

"Whatever. I like my job.''

"So do I. Or at least I need it.'' Maggie's face brightened. "Three more payments and the house is mine. Do you think I'll make it?''

"After today, I'm not so sure.''

"Karen....''

"Sorry, but you attract trouble like a magnet.''

Maggie sighed, pulling at the short bow tie around her neck like it was a rope about to strangle her. "Now you sound like my father. He just can't get it through his head that I can handle my own life. He keeps calling me and telling me to come home, but the base in Texas is no more home to me than the dozens of other places we've lived in.'' She shook her head in frustration. "That's why this house is so important. I am determined to prove I can make a real home for myself—something my mother would have liked.''

Maggie paused, feeling the familiar emotional tug that never seemed to go away, even though it had been years since her mother's death. "I am going to be the perfect domestic goddess or whatever they call home-makers these days.''

Karen smiled at her friend's enthusiasm. "I wish you luck. Personally, I'd rather have a maid, a cook and a gardener than do any of that stuff myself. But if you think it will make you happy, more power to you. I wish you luck."

"And no more problems here," Maggie added. "Mr. Stone loves to put a black mark on my time card whenever he can."

"Then just stay out of trouble."

"I'd like to do that, but it gets tough when complete strangers walk off the street and kiss me."

Karen burst out laughing. "By the way, what room did you give our illustrious guest?"

"Room 316."

"Why?"

"Mr. Stone insisted. I think he's hoping for a short stay."

"What's our mystery man's name? Just in case he calls the desk."

"J. Hollister. He said his friends call him Jake."

"And are you going to be his *friend?*"

"Not on your life. That man is trouble. I hope I never see him again." Maggie turned away from Karen and self-consciously touched her fingers to her lips. She could still feel the tingle, the excitement, the sense of imminent danger. Jake Hollister had turned her world upside down in one long, passionate kiss. Thirty seconds of heat. She had gotten a taste of that elusive something she had always wondered about but had never really felt, not even when she had tried desperately to convince herself she was in love with the "right man."

Not that Jake was anywhere near to being the right man. He was wrong in every way imaginable. He kissed like an outlaw, and she was looking for a good guy.

Jake stretched out on the bed, raising his arms over his head and letting the tension unwind from his stiff muscles. So much for the freedom of a motorcycle. He felt as if he'd been on horseback for three days straight. Muscles he didn't even know he had were aching.

Still, it was a good ache. Physical exertion and the pain of exercise had helped block out the other pain for over a year now. As long as he kept moving, he could stay ahead of it.

He closed his eyes, thinking about the happy oblivion of sleep. Yet, instead of seeing the welcoming cocoon of darkness, he saw a cloud of dark brown hair, light blue eyes and a soft, open mouth. He smiled to himself. The look on her face had been priceless.

He had kissed her for a lark. She had look so damned straitlaced in her navy blue skirt, white shirt and button-down vest. When he had walked up to the desk, she had been polite and cool, eyeing him as if he were a bug crawling across her precious marble floor. He had wanted to shake her up, and he had.

So, go to sleep, he told himself, but her face kept floating in front of his eyes, and he absentmindedly rubbed the back of his hand across his mouth. Her kiss had been more than he bargained for. He had expected her to yank away, not kiss him back with such warm, spontaneous generosity. Maybe he had misjudged her. After all, appearances could be deceiving. He knew that better than anyone.

The phone next to the bed rang. He opened his eyes with a groan. Stretching across the bed, he lifted the receiver. "Yeah?"

"Yeah? Is that the way your mother taught you to answer the phone?" The woman's voice was sharp and stern and brought a smile to his lips.

"Aunt Ida. You must have ESP. I just checked in."

"Not ESP, just an ear to the ground. You caused quite a stir in my lobby. How are you, dear?"

He yawned and then laughed. "Tired. I drove up from L.A. today. It was quite a ride." He stuffed a pillow more comfortably under his head, knowing his aunt's penchant for long chats.

"A motorcycle? Oh, my," she said.

"It suits me. I'm a rambling man these days. You know that."

"I do, and sometimes I think I'd like to join you. So when are you going to give me a ride on that beast?"

The sparkle in her voice made him smile at the thought of his sixty-seven-year-old aunt hanging on to his waist as they careened around a corner. The rest of the family would be horrified, but she would probably love it. He shook the image out of his mind as Ida jumped back into conversation.

"I'm dying to see you, honey. I want to talk about our plans. I have some marvelous ideas. I know you're going to love them."

"Wait just a minute." He scrambled up on the bed, knowing he better have his wits about him, or Ida would talk him into something he didn't want to do. She had a kind of infectious enthusiasm that made people believe in impossible dreams. "I told you I'd come up here to see you and check out your operation, but nothing long-term. You understand that, don't you? I'm leaving in ten days."

"Of course you are."

"Aunt Ida," he said warningly. "Don't get any ideas about pulling me deeper into the family business. I like being a troubleshooter. I get to travel all over the country and never see the same people twice."

"Some people are worth seeing twice," Ida replied, sending a long-suffering sigh over the receiver that didn't fool him for a minute. "But I'm not going to push. At least we can have some fun while you're here. Although I think you may have started without me. Did you really kiss my front-desk clerk?"

Jake chuckled, remembering the look on the desk clerk's face when he'd kissed her. "Guilty."

"You're a bad boy."

"And I've been punished with the worst room in the hotel." Jake looked around the room as he spoke. It wasn't that bad. At least he had a queen-size bed and cable television to catch the sports update. Although he was sure there had to be some hidden annoyances. After spending the past year traveling to each of the Castleton hotels and some of their competition's, he had a good idea where most of the skeletons were hidden.

"I'm sorry about that," Ida continued. "Maybe next time you'll behave yourself. Besides, I thought you weren't interested in women anymore."

"On a short-term basis they're okay."

There was a long silence, and Jake knew that Ida was an expert at reading between the lines. She was the only one in the family who came close to understanding him. Maybe that's why he hadn't come to her hotel during the past year. She would want to know how he was feeling about Carole, and he wasn't sure anymore. Grief and anger had turned to confusion and self-examination. The relationship with his ex-wife had taken on a dreamlike quality, and he didn't know what he felt anymore. The only thing he was certain of was that he didn't want to discuss his feelings with his aunt.

"Why don't I give you a call later?" Jake said quickly. "I'm really bushed."

"Of course. We'll have dinner. I know a wonderful restaurant that serves Thai food. I think you'll love it."

"If you say so. But is this place somewhere out of the way? I thought you wanted me to be incognito. What if someone sees us together?"

Ida laughed, a rich, lively sound that warmed his soul. "They'll probably think I'm having a wild affair with a younger man. I can't wait. I'll let you go, dear, but before I do, any questions?"

"Just one." He paused, debating the wisdom of his words.

"Her name is Maggie Gordon, but don't get any ideas about her."

He stared up at the ceiling in disgust, annoyed that she could read him so easily. "Why not? You usually like to throw eligible women in front of me. Is she married or something?"

"No, but she's different. You wouldn't be able to leave her in ten days, and I know you don't want to change your plans."

Jake laughed. "You're waving a red flag right in my face. There's not a woman alive who could make me want to stay in one place—not ever again."

Ida sighed. "You remind me so much of myself."

"How so?"

"I used to think I knew everything, too."

Chapter Two

Maggie walked into the office behind the front desk and picked her time card out of the slot. Pushing it into the clock, she punched out and turned to leave.

"Maggie. I'm so glad I caught you."

"Mrs. Castleton." Maggie smiled at the petite, energetic woman standing in front of her. Ida Castleton was a beautiful older woman with stark white hair and sparkling gray eyes. Today, she was dressed in black stretch pants and an oversize bright pink sweater that brought out the roses in her cheeks. If Mrs. Castleton wasn't the owner of the hotel and her employer, they probably could have been good friends. As it was, Maggie tried to maintain a respectful distance.

"I need your help, dear," Ida said.

Maggie looked at her in surprise. "Me? What can I do?"

"You can start by following me outside." Ida tipped her head, directing Maggie's gaze toward the inner office where Harry Stone was conversing with one of the other employees. "I need a little privacy."

Puzzled by Ida's request, Maggie could do nothing but agree. "That sounds easy enough."

They walked out of the office and down the hall to a side door that led into the garden area, the quietest of the three courtyards. In the center was a beautiful stone cupid astride a fountain that sprayed an impressive jet of water against the blue and black tiles at its base. The flowers surrounding the courtyard were blooming gloriously under the warm September sunshine.

Ida led her past a group of women playing bridge at one of the tables that surrounded the courtyard and finally sat down on an oak bench at the other end of the yard. She patted the spot next to her, and Maggie joined her.

"This is my favorite spot," Ida said, taking a deep whiff of the floral-scented air. "I almost feel like I'm in my own garden instead of a courtyard surrounded by two hundred bedrooms."

"That's part of the charm of the Castleton," Maggie said. "It's a lot like home. Or in some cases, better than home."

Ida smiled and patted her leg. "I have a favor to ask of you, Maggie."

Maggie sent the older woman a curious look. "Of course, I'm happy to help you."

"Good. My nephew is in town, and he's a wonderful boy, but I find I just don't have the energy to take him around and show him the sights." Ida sighed wearily. "My age is catching up with me, you know."

Maggie looked at her doubtfully, remembering two days earlier when she had seen her playing tennis with one of the resident pros.

"I hate to impose, but would you show him around a bit? You have tomorrow off, don't you?"

"Yes." Maggie said the word reluctantly, thinking of all the things she had planned for Saturday. But Mrs. Castleton rarely asked her for anything. How could she refuse such a simple request?

"I'd be happy to compensate you for the time."

"You don't have to do that. I can give up a few hours to help you out. What does he want to do?"

Ida waved an idle hand. "A little of everything. Whatever takes his fancy or yours."

Maggie nodded and forced a smile on her face. "What time?"

"Nine o'clock until about twelve. Or you can see how it goes."

"That sounds fine. What room is he in?"

"The number escapes me right now. Why don't I have him meet you at your house. I'll drop him off first thing."

"I can't wait," Maggie muttered.

Mrs. Castleton smiled and stood up. "Neither can I."

The next morning, Jake stepped off the private elevator that led to his aunt's suite and knocked on the door. It was half past eight, and he was grumpy and hungry, his usual state in the morning.

"Hello, honey," Ida said cheerfully as she opened the door. She stood on tiptoe and gave him a kiss on his stubbly cheek. Then she shook a finger at him. "Did you forget to shave?"

"No, I didn't forget. This is the new me."

"Well, come in, anyway. I have a surprise for you."

Jake halted halfway through the door. "I don't think I like your surprises."

"But this one is good." Ida took his hand and pulled him farther into the room. "When we were talking last night, I got to thinking about how best to use your sharp eye, and I think I have a plan. I don't want Mr. Stone to know who you are, at least not yet, and frankly, today is going to be a very busy day in the hotel. We have a church convention with every ladies' group in Northern California getting together here."

Jake looked at her, wondering where this was all leading. "What does that have to do with me?"

"I'd like you to disappear for a while. This group wouldn't be too thrilled with someone like you, and I can't afford to lose the business."

"And?" he prodded, waiting for the other shoe to drop.

"I thought this would be a good time for you to see the surrounding area. There are major local attractions that you should investigate."

Jake stared at her for a long moment, wishing he could read her as easily as she could read him. "Fine. I'll take off for the day and meet up with you tonight. But first I'm going to snatch a quick breakfast in the dining room."

Ida grabbed on to the sleeve of his T-shirt. "The church ladies have an early-morning breakfast. They're in the dining room now."

"Then tell me where the nearest doughnut shop is, and I'll get out of your hair."

"One-twenty-five Paloma. I'll give you directions."

Jake's eyes narrowed thoughtfully. "You know the address to the doughnut shop?"

Ida laughed. "Of course not. I've arranged for you to meet one of my friends. She's going to show you around today. I want you to be polite. She's a nice woman."

"You hooked me up with one of your lady friends?" He ran a hand through his hair. "Do I have to change and shave?"

"Only if you want to."

"I don't."

"Then go as you are. I don't want to make things difficult for you."

"Right. I just have to get out of the hotel and spend the day being nice to someone I've never met." Jake shook his head warningly. "I'll do this, but no more plans, please. I'm here to check out operations in the hotel, and if you're not going to let me do that, I'll call Uncle Bill and tell him his sister is being difficult."

"My brother may oversee the chain, but around here I'm the boss." Ida pushed him out the door of her suite. "Thanks, honey, I really appreciate this. See you tonight."

Paloma Street was not what Jake had expected. Set on the outskirts of Napa, the houses were on the small side, some run-down, others in the midst of remodeling. It looked like a neighborhood in a state of change, and he couldn't imagine one of his aunt's cronies living in such a place. Although Ida wasn't a snob, her moneyed status seemed to attract other wealthy women.

At least his motorcycle didn't look out of place in this neighborhood. On one side of the street, he saw a group of teenagers working on an old car, and he smiled to himself as their envious looks followed him down the street.

A few years ago he would not have thought twice about impressing a bunch of kids with the roar of a motorcycle. Entrepreneurs and big-business CEOs had been his targets then. If Carole could see him now, she'd be horrified. He'd certainly come a long way from his days of expensive Italian suits, car phones and deal-making.

Some of his friends would say he'd gone down—way down, and maybe he had, but it sure felt a lot better to have the sun on his skin and the wind at his back than to be sitting in an office twelve hours a day making another buck to spend on something he wouldn't have time to enjoy.

No, this was definitely the life. No strings, no attachments, no messy personal relationships . . . and nothing to tie him down. He was not going to get caught up in the trap of commitment ever again. He had learned his lesson well.

Veering over to the side of the street, he checked a number on the curb and then pulled back onto the road. The numbers were definitely going down into the hundreds and the houses were getting farther apart as the neighborhood began to take on a more countrified look. In the back of one yard, he spotted a few horses and in the back of another, a coop full of chickens.

Aunt Ida had a friend living here? He was beginning to get an uneasy feeling in the pit of his stomach, but it was too late to back out. He'd come this far; he might as well go the rest of the way.

The last block ended in a cul-de-sac, fringed with a thick patch of tall eucalyptus trees. The sun filtered through the branches in long golden rays, and he could hear birds singing even over the roar of his bike. He felt like an intruder, as if he should have come on horseback instead of on a machine.

One-twenty-five was the last house on the street. It was painted bright white with blue shutters adorning the windows. There were rows of colorful flowers along the curb and in planters leading up to the front steps. A new wooden fence ran along the driveway, and Jake took the turn a little faster than he should have. Although he'd gotten used to the bike on his long ride up from L.A., he still wasn't an expert, and the wheelbarrow in the middle of the driveway took him completely by surprise.

Swearing under his breath, he pulled the bike viciously to the right, and hung on tight as the powerful machine ran off the driveway, through a garden and finally came to rest on the middle of the front lawn. He hoped Aunt Ida's friend had a sense of humor.

The front door opened, followed by a feminine shriek of alarm and the sound of the screen door banging in disapproval. He winced to himself and slowly turned his head, prepared to offer a heartfelt apology.

"Oh my God, you've killed Henry." Maggie flung her hands to her cheeks in dismay as she stared at the vegetable garden that was now gaping with motorcycle tracks.

Jake opened his mouth to say something and then stopped. Who the hell was Henry? He got off his bike, pulled the helmet off his head and slid off his sunglasses so he could take a better look. The driveway was empty, save for the wheelbarrow he'd barely missed hitting and a bright orange Volkswagen. He turned to look at the woman, and his gaze connected with a pair of indignant blue eyes. Maggie stared at him in shock. "You?"

Jake smiled as the pieces of the puzzle fell into place. "What a coincidence, huh?"

"I can't believe it's you."

Maggie shook her head in bewilderment and blinked her eyes hard as if she were hoping he'd disappear. Actually, it wasn't a bad idea; Aunt Ida's plan was not going to work anyway. "Look—" he began, only to be cut off by her anger.

"No, you look. First, you nearly get me fired and now you kill Henry."

Jake looked over at the path his motorcyle had taken and then back into her furious face. "I don't see any bodies."

She shook her head in disgust and marched over to the garden. Squatting down, she pulled at one of the long vines. "Maybe you missed him. I hope to God you missed him, because there is no way I could grow another one like him in a week."

Jake walked over to join her, staring hard at what looked to him like a bunch of zucchini set off by bright yellow flowers. He squatted down beside her to take a closer look. "Am I missing something here? Who is Henry?"

"My prize zucchini," Maggie said sharply, as her fingers explored the thick vines of the plant. When she came in contact with the smooth green skin of her best vegetable, she let out a sigh of relief and moved the leaves aside so he could see it. "You missed him, after all. This is Henry."

Jake looked down at the largest zucchini he had ever seen in his life and scratched his head in bewilderment. "Do you always name your vegetables?"

Maggie gave the zucchini a loving pat. "Only my favorites, and this one is very, very special. He's going to win me a blue ribbon in the county fair next week."

Jake stared at her, just as puzzled after her explanation as he had been before. "You entered the county fair? I thought that was for farmers."

"No, of course not. Anybody can enter. I'm also in the apple pie competition. I'm going to use my grandmother's recipe, but judging by my last two pie efforts, I think I have a better chance to win a ribbon with Henry."

Jake nodded, rubbing his chin thoughtfully. She was a gorgeous woman but completely loony. "Whatever you say."

Maggie frowned down at the plant. "I just hope the trauma of having your motorcycle almost run him over won't stunt Henry's growth."

Jake smiled and then grinned and finally burst out laughing. "Maybe you should send old Hank to a zucchini doctor just to be sure there are no long-lasting effects."

Maggie turned her head and sent him a disgusted look. "You obviously don't appreciate good vegetables."

"Of course I do, every time I put one in my mouth. I'll bet Hank would be mighty tasty. What do you say we just pick him up and plop him in a pot of boiling water?"

Jake teasingly reached for the zucchini, and Maggie grabbed his wrist. "Don't you dare touch him."

Her abrupt movement made her lose her balance, and she tumbled into the side of him, knocking him over at the same time. Suddenly, she was sprawled across a masculine chest, her fingers coming to rest on the rapidly beating pulse in his neck. It was racing as fast as her heart, and when she looked into his eyes, she drew in a long, slow breath.

He had looked good before, even with his rough shadow of beard, but up close, the light green eyes sparkled against his tanned skin, and the planes of his face were strong and bold. The tiny gold earring he wore dared her to explore, and instinct sent her hand to the side of his face. She traced the line of his jaw and then pulled gently on the earring, watching in fascination as the look in his eyes darkened into something very, very dangerous.

Jake cupped her face with his hands, his thumbs moving in a circular pattern against her cheekbones. His touch was hot and sensuous, pulling her closer. In another second, she would be kissing him. Good Lord! What was she doing?

Maggie sat up in haste, pushing her hair nervously back behind one ear. "I wish you hadn't done that."

Jake sat up, rubbing the dirt off the sleeves of his leather jacket. "You were the one who tackled me."

"Only because you were threatening Henry."

"Really? I thought you just wanted to kiss me again."

"No. Absolutely not." Maggie jumped to her feet before the urge to do just that turned her into a liar.

"Help me up, babe," he said, holding out his hand.

"I'm not your babe." She crossed her arms in front of her waist. She didn't want to touch him again. Even the simplest move with this guy seemed to get her into trouble.

"Afraid?"

Years of responding to her brother's dares made her reach out her hand and take his. The brief contact sent a jolt down her spine, and as soon as he was on his feet, she immediately let go, sliding it into the pocket of her blue jeans for good measure.

"What are you doing here, anyway?" Maggie demanded. "Hoping to fine-tune your driving skills on a deserted road?"

"Hardly. I would have been okay if you hadn't left your wheelbarrow in the middle of the driveway."

"I was going to move it before..." Maggie's voice drifted away as her gaze sharpened. "That still doesn't explain why you're here."

"I was told to come here by my Aunt Ida."

"Your Aunt Ida?" Maggie emphasized each word, hoping she was hearing him wrong.

"That's right, Ida Castleton."

"You're her nephew? She said you were a little boy." Maggie paused in confusion. "At least I think she said that. Maybe I misunderstood."

"I doubt it. This is just like her."

"What is just like her?"

"Setting me up with a single, attractive, eligible woman." Jake drawled the words, enjoying the sudden nervous look in her eyes. He watched as her hand crept up to her necklace, and she slid the gold heart back and forth on the chain while she tried to think of something to say.

"But I'm not—"

"Not what? Single?"

"I am single, but—"

"Not attractive? Have you looked in the mirror lately?"

Maggie cleared her throat. "Why would your aunt think I would be interested in you? You embarrassed me yesterday and today you nearly killed—"

"Hank, I know."

"Would you stop interrupting me?"

"Look, forget about yesterday and this morning. I'm starving and I could use a cup of hot, strong coffee, along with a big stack of hot cakes. You got anything on the stove?" he asked hopefully.

Maggie looked at him in amazement. "You want me to cook you breakfast? Why on earth should I?"

"Because I'm hungry."

"Then go to a coffee shop." Maggie started to walk away, but he caught her by the arm.

"You're the one who agreed to entertain me."

"That's when I thought you were a kid."

"I'm still her nephew."

Maggie hesitated, comprehending the subtle pressure of his words. "Fine. If you want a cup of coffee, I'll get you one." A small smile tugged at the corner of her mouth. "And maybe you'd like to try my apple pie."

Maggie set the cup of steaming coffee on the kitchen table and watched as Jake took a greedy whiff. "It's French mocha. I hope it isn't too strong. I have a tendency to put in a little more than necessary."

Jake lifted the cup to his lips and took a sip, his mouth puckering as the strong liquid slid down his throat. "Perfect, just the way I like it."

"Good." Maggie took a drink, as well, and a long silence fell between them. She tried to think of something to say, but nothing came to mind. It had been a long time since she'd had a man in for coffee, and they'd certainly never been wearing snakeskin boots and leather jackets.

"Nice place," Jake commented, taking a look around the cozy kitchen. It was a medium-size room with cheerful yellow curtains and colorful magnets on the refrigerator, nothing like the kitchen he'd grown up in or the one Carole had personally designed for the mansion in Beverly Hills. He decided he liked this one better.

She smiled at the compliment. "It's coming along. Three more payments, and it's all mine, or at least I'll have the down payment." She paused, wondering why on earth she was confiding her financial problems to a complete stranger.

"So, you want to own a house?" Jake said, imbuing the words with a twist of irony.

"Yes, a place that is all mine."

"And you'll have to kill yourself to keep it that way."

Maggie looked at the grim smile on his face and wondered what had brought on such a strong reaction. "Why do you say that?" she asked.

"Because you'll be chaining yourself to a heavy mortgage, a prisoner of whatever job it takes to make the payments. You won't be able to do what you want when you want because you'll always be thinking of ways to make another buck."

Maggie studied him thoughtfully over the rim of her coffee cup. "You make it sound pretty bad. Do you have your own place?"

He shook his head. "Not anymore. I have an apartment in Los Angeles, but most of the time I'm on the road."

"Doing what?"

"This and that. Enough to buy my next meal."

"Oh." Maggie fell silent, not sure what to say. She'd rarely met a man who didn't have a job or didn't at least pretend to want one.

"How do you like your job at the hotel?" he asked, breaking into her thoughts.

The mention of the hotel made her sit up straighter as she remembered exactly why he was sitting in her kitchen. She needed her job to make her payments, and unfortunately he was her boss's nephew.

"It's wonderful. The guests are interesting and come from all over the world. The setting is beautiful, and I make a good living."

"Nice sales pitch. What about the people you work with? I don't think you and old Stoneface hit it off too well."

Maggie dropped her gaze to the black liquid in her cup and hid a smile. Harry Stone definitely fit his name. "He's okay. I can handle him."

"Is that why you let him give me the worst room in the place?"

She tipped her head. "Some things aren't worth fighting for, and I wasn't feeling in a very charitable mood at the time. If you have a problem, you should talk to Mr. Stone. I'm sure he doesn't know you're Mrs. Castleton's nephew."

"I'm sure he doesn't, not that it should make a difference." Jake paused, looking around the room again. "Did I hear you say something about apple pie? I haven't had breakfast yet, and I do love home cooking."

She looked at him and hesitated, wondering what Mrs. Castleton would do if her nephew came down with food poisoning. She should offer him some of the store-bought doughnuts she had in the cupboard. He might be a little on the obnoxious side, but he probably didn't deserve her apple pie.

"You didn't really bake a pie, did you?" he asked with a sardonic smile. "That's okay. You can give me one out of your freezer. My ex-wife was great at re-heating."

Irritation filled her at his smug tone. Getting up from her chair, she walked over to the counter and unveiled the pie. Taking a knife out of the drawer, she carried the pie over to the table. "Here it is."

Jake looked at the knife in her hand and pushed his chair down along the edge of the table. "Make sure you don't miss, honey."

Maggie smiled and cut an imaginary path through the air with the knife. Then she placed it on the pie and cut a slice. Pushing the plate over to him, she sat down in her chair and waited for him to take a bite.

Jake picked up his fork. "Doesn't look too bad." He took a bite and started to chew. His eyes bulged out, and he moved his mouth in a rapid motion, finally swallowing hard. "My God! What's in that thing? Motor oil?" He reached for his coffee and took a long drink.

"You mean you don't like it?"

He gave her a sharp look. "You knew I wouldn't. It tastes like sour lemons."

She shrugged her shoulders. "I did take a bite earlier. But at least we both know it didn't come from a store. I don't play games, Mr. Hollister."

"You also don't cook."

"I found my grandmother's recipe on three pieces of paper in grease-smudged handwriting. No one got her to write it down until she was eighty, and I think she left something out. I haven't been able to figure out what. But I'm going to get it right, even if it kills me."

"It just might."

Maggie frowned. "I can't believe you're really re-lated to Mrs. Castleton. She's so sweet. Although, it wasn't very nice of her to set me up with you. I wonder why she did it?'' Maggie paused, folding her arms on the table as she studied him. "Can't you get a date?''

"Of course I can get a date,'' he said in annoyance. "This was not my idea. For some reason, she thought the two of us would hit it off.''

"I can't imagine why,'' Maggie said, letting her gaze travel over his face, down to his jacket and blue jeans. Actually, it was pretty easy to imagine why. Jake Hollister was one of the finest-looking men she'd ever met. It was too bad he didn't have a personality to match.

Jake sat back in his chair and returned the appraisal. Maggie shifted uneasily under his gaze. She knew she was reasonably attractive, but for some reason his long stare was making her decidedly edgy, as if it were important that he found her attractive. But it definitely wasn't. It didn't matter what he thought of her, because they were not going to go any further than coffee in her kitchen.

Jake pushed back his chair and stood up. "Thanks for the coffee, but I'm going to push off now.''

"I thought we were going to spend the morning together.'' The words came out of her mouth before she could stop them. She didn't want to spend hours with him. Another minute in his company would be too long.

Jake shook his head. "I don't think so.''

Maggie hesitated. Keeping her job was still the bottom line, even if it meant putting up with this man. "Wait. I think we should do something.''

Jake raised his eyebrow in surprise. "Why?''

"Because your aunt went to a lot of trouble to set this up. We shouldn't disappoint her.''

Jake's eyes narrowed as he stared at her, and Maggie felt a sense of unease. "What's wrong?'' she asked.

"You just said you don't play games."

"I don't."

"You mean you're not going out with me to please the boss? Of course you are. You're terrified I'm going to report you and she's going to put you out on your sweet little butt before you get the down payment for this house."

It was so close to the truth, Maggie was speechless. She wanted to explain that he didn't understand how much the house meant to her, how long she'd been working for it. But he wasn't going to give her a chance to say anything.

"You're just like everyone else," he added. "You can be had for the right price. I wonder..."

"What?" she asked sharply.

"Just how far you're willing to go."

Chapter Three

"Out. Get out, right now," Maggie ordered, pointing her finger to the kitchen door. "Move it, mister."

Jake didn't move a muscle, but his face lightened at her response. "Truth hurts, doesn't it?"

"If you want to report me to Mrs. Castleton, then go right ahead. I don't care. I was simply trying to be nice."

"How nice?"

"Certainly not what you're thinking. I don't have a price, Mr. Hollister. And I cannot be had. So take your motorcycle and your attitude and get out of here."

"I don't think so."

"Look, I don't want to get nasty, but—"

"But what?" he asked with interest. "What are you going to do? Call the cops? Are you afraid I'm going to touch you?" He stretched out his arm and caressed her cheek with his fingers, a searing touch that made her hot and angry.

"You're asking for it," she said warningly, knocking his arm away with her hand. "I don't want you to touch me."

"Are you sure about that?"

He slid his arms around her waist and pulled her up against his body. Her legs tangled between his strong, muscular thighs, and for a moment, she almost forgot to fight.

"What are you doing?" she asked furiously.

"Nothing yet."

"That's it," she said.

With a twist of her body and a skillful, well-practiced move, she grasped his arm, turned her back to him and flipped him onto the floor. He landed with a thud and an agonized groan as he grabbed his right wrist.

"What the hell did you do that for?"

"I told you to get out," Maggie said, feeling a twinge of guilt at the flash of pain across his face. Seeing the look of fury in his eyes, she took another step back and crossed her arms around her waist. "Are you okay?"

"No, I'm not. Help me up."

She stared at him indecisively, then offered him a hand. Jake's fingers twined around hers in a bone-crushing grip. He pulled her down on the floor so fast she was breathless. Suddenly, she was on her back, her chest crushed by the weight of Jake's body as he sprawled over her.

"Now, where were we?" he asked.

"You tricked me. I was trying to be nice."

"Really? Was that before or after you flipped me? By the way, where did you learn to do that?"

Maggie squirmed under his weight. "My father is a colonel in the marines, and I have three older brothers. They taught me how to defend myself."

"But not to run like hell afterward," Jake commented. "Next time you do that to a man, you might want to head for the hills."

"I thought you were hurt. Let me up."

"I will . . . eventually."

"Jake, please."

"I like the way you say that." His lips twisted into a wry smile. "But how do I know I can trust you not to go after me again?"

"I won't."

"I was only having a little fun. I would never hurt you. And I will take no for an answer, but..." His voice turned husky, and his gaze drifted down from her eyes to her mouth. "I was thinking about the other day and how good it felt to kiss you."

Maggie stared at him, mesmerized by the tone of his voice, the sultry longing in his words. It would be so easy to get taken in by him, to forget about everything that mattered to her. But at what price? She had worked too hard to let herself get distracted now by the kind of man who probably wouldn't stick around till the morning, much less the day after or the rest of her life.

Jake's head swooped down and his lips touched the curve of her cheek, drifting over to the corner of her mouth. His tongue teased along the edge of her lip. He was giving her plenty of time to say no, so why was she suddenly mute? And why was she rolling around the kitchen floor with a man she barely knew?

Maggie pressed her hands against his chest and gave Jake an abrupt and hearty shove, taking him completely by surprise. He rolled over on one side, groaning as his sore hand took the weight of his body.

"That's enough," she said, jumping to her feet. "I must be crazy."

Jake groaned and closed his eyes. "I won't argue with that. You have a friend who's a zucchini, you whip up poison apple pies and you can probably kill a man with your bare hands. What on earth was my aunt thinking?"

"I just thought the two of you would enjoy each other's company," Ida Castleton said, giving Maggie an innocent look. "I'm very sorry if I put you in an awkward position."

Ida walked across the living room of her elegant suite to a silver tea service sitting on the table. She poured herself a cup and then looked inquiringly at Maggie. "Would you like some tea, dear?"

"No, thank you, I'm fine."

Ida set the pitcher down and stirred some sugar into her tea. "I should have been English. I always enjoy a cup of tea in the late afternoon. The Castleton Hotel in London serves up the most delicious tea with homemade scones. You have to see it to believe it."

"Maybe someday I will," Maggie said, trying to think of a way to get Mrs. Castleton back to the subject at hand. She had spent all day Saturday trying to find a delicate way out of her problem, but nothing had come to her. She had even gone to church this morning, hoping for divine intervention, but here it was Sunday afternoon and she was no closer to finding a diplomatic way to say "butt out" than she had been yesterday.

"Of course you will," Ida continued, interrupting Maggie's thoughts "See the London hotel, that is," she added as Maggie looked at her blankly.

"Oh, right."

"Castleton employees are often transferred, especially if we know someone has an interest in another location." Ida crossed the room and sat down on the sofa across from Maggie. "If you could go anywhere in the world, where would it be?"

Maggie smiled at the question. "Right here. The Napa Valley of Northern California. It's beautiful and the weather is great. I can't imagine a nicer spot."

"You're really that content here?" Ida asked with genuine interest.

"Yes. I've moved around my entire life. By the time I was in the fifth grade, I'd been to seven different schools."

"That must have been difficult for you."

"I managed. My mom was great at making a home wherever we went," Maggie said, feeling a touch of sadness at the memory. "I remember one house was old and falling apart. My mom looked at it and put this beautiful smile on her face, even though I had the feeling she was about to burst out crying. Then she rolled up her sleeves and said, 'Let's get to work.' By the end of the week, that place was warm and homey. She was a miracle worker."

"You sound sad when you talk about her," Ida commented.

"She died when I was eleven. Sometimes it still hurts."

"Of course it does. Losing someone close to you is never easy to accept, no matter what the relationship was."

"I guess. Anyway, that's why I want to stay right here and make my own home. It's time. It's long past time."

Ida set down her cup on the saucer. "Does that mean you're thinking of settling down with someone in particular?"

Maggie smiled to herself. "No. I'm going to do this by myself."

"But why? Surely a young woman like you would have dozens of men eager to share a home with you."

A bed, maybe. A home didn't seem to be too high on anyone's list of priorities except hers. "No one at the moment, and that's okay," she said. "It's nice to be able to make plans that don't have to please anyone but me."

Maggie leaned back against the chair, sliding her fingers along the embroidered arms. Everything in Mrs. Castleton's private suite was luxuriously expensive and rich in beauty. Mrs. Castleton fit in perfectly, but she couldn't imagine Jake sitting anywhere in this room. "Mrs. Castleton, we need to talk about your nephew."

Ida sighed. "I was afraid you were going to say that. I know he can be a bit of a troublemaker, but he's a good boy at heart."

He was a big troublemaker and he certainly wasn't a boy, Maggie thought, but she wasn't going to say that to his aunt. "Your nephew and I don't seem to have a lot in common."

"Oh, I think you're wrong. Jake has just had some personal problems in his life that shaped some of his current attitudes."

Maggie sat up straight in her chair. "What happened?"

"I really couldn't say. I'll have to let Jake tell you that. Just keep in mind that what you see on the outside isn't necessarily what's on the inside. What I want to know is how he hurt his wrist. He said something about taking a fall in your kitchen, but he was very evasive. In fact, he almost seemed embarrassed.''

"He tripped over something,'' Maggie replied, unable to meet the direct query in the older woman's eyes. She had hurt the man's arm and his ego, there was no point in taking it any further. "I feel terrible that your nephew got injured on my property, but I really wish you would have leveled with me. You knew that I thought your nephew was a little boy."

"I suppose I did, but I had a feeling you wouldn't go if I told you the truth.''

"Probably not. Your nephew doesn't follow the same rules I do.''

"I know. He tends to make them up as he goes along. If you get to know him . . .''

Maggie held up a hand to stop her. "I think you should leave that decision up to us.''

"You're right. But that leaves me with a small problem.'' Ida took a sip of tea and smiled helplessly. "I want you to take Jake wine-tasting tomorrow.''

"What?'' Maggie asked in amazement.

"Wine-tasting. We have some of the most wonderful wineries in the world here in the Napa Valley and over in Sonoma. I want him to select some new wines for our cellar. I'm thinking of expanding our selection.''

"But you have a wine buyer.''

"I do, but Jake is family, and he knows my tastes.''

Maggie stared at Mrs. Castleton, unable to believe that the woman was still intent on throwing them together after everything she had said. "Maybe I didn't make myself clear.''

"Oh, you did, and I won't plan anything else, I promise. The problem is Jake. He's not just here to visit me. He's going to help me get this hotel into tip-top shape. We've been losing business the past few months, and I can't figure out why. Jake is going to review my operations. He'll tell me where the cracks are, how I can improve my efficiency and service, attract more tourists and even locals who may want a romantic getaway weekend."

Maggie sent her a doubtful look. Jake, the biker, was going to do all that? "Does he know the hotel business?"

"Yes, among other things." Ida leaned forward, dropping her voice down, so that Maggie had to move closer to hear her. "I'll let you in on another secret, Maggie. I've known Jake since he was a baby, and I've seen him go through all kinds of phases. But underneath it all, he's a very special man. If you take the trouble to get to know him, I think you'll find it's worth your while."

"I'm sure he's nice," Maggie said with a placating smile. "But the two of us really don't get along. In fact, I don't think he likes me at all."

Ida laughed and got to her feet. "Why don't we find out? Do this for me, dear. I know it's an imposition, but I really do need your help. I'll pay you overtime. You're working the night shift tomorrow, so perhaps during the day you could take him to some wineries?"

Maggie sighed. "I shouldn't let you get away with this."

"I know, but say you'll go."

"Even if I say yes, I would not be at all surprised if Jake said no."

"Leave him to me. And remember, Maggie. This is our secret. I don't want Mr. Stone or any of the other clerks to know who Jake really is. It would be very dif-

ficult for him to do an honest appraisal of the hotel if
people were putting on a show for him.''

''Aren't you afraid I'll do the same thing?''

Ida shook her head and smiled. ''Did you know he
was my nephew when he—slipped—in your kitchen?''

''Yes.''

''Then, I don't think I have anything to worry
about.''

Maybe Mrs. Castleton didn't have anything to worry
about, but Maggie certainly did. Like what it was going to feel like to spend the entire day with Jake, a man
who sent her blood pressure skyrocketing every time he
looked at her. She had never felt such an intensity of
emotions for a man—not even Mark, who had nearly
talked her into walking down the aisle with him.

It was ridiculous to get so worked up over someone
who was the antithesis of everything she wanted. He
was a tough guy, a biker, maybe even a bum. And he
kissed like the devil. Shaking her head, she got out of
her car and walked around to the front of the hotel
where she was supposed to meet Jake.

This was going to have to be it. One trip through the
wine country and she would tell Mrs. Castleton to find
someone else to show her nephew around.

The driveway in front of the hotel was empty and the
valet was talking to one of the bellhops as Maggie
walked over to the curb. There was no sign of Jake.
Looking at her watch, Maggie frowned. It was ten
o'clock. Mrs. Castleton had said he would be in front
of the hotel at exactly ten. She would give him five
minutes and then turn around and go home. There were
certainly dozens of other things she could do with her
day. It was going to be hot and sunny, a perfect time for

gardening. Or she could try another apple pie. She had to get at least one right before the fair opened on Friday.

The roar of an engine coming out of the hotel parking garage made every muscle in her body tighten up, until her neck was almost too stiff to turn. Finally, she managed.

The black-and-silver bike was slick, sophisticated and fast, matching its driver perfectly. Jake was dressed the same as the day before in blue jeans and boots, but he had foregone the black leather jacket; instead, he wore a light blue T-shirt that showed the ripple of muscle in his upper arms and a strong, flat chest upon which was emblazoned the words *Party Animal*.

Maggie felt another surge of wariness. What on earth was she getting herself into? This man was out of her league. He wasn't smiling today, either. His sparkling green eyes were hidden by a pair of sunglasses, and a shaggy edge of curls crept out from beneath his helmet. His jaw was stiff and stern, square and uncompromising. At the moment, he looked more like her father than a party animal. He seemed to be a man of many moods.

"Ready?" Jake prompted in a deep voice. Without waiting for an answer, he pulled an extra helmet out of the side storage compartment.

"I'm not getting on that," Maggie said immediately.

"Yes, you are."

He tossed the helmet to her. She grabbed it awkwardly before it could fall to the ground.

"This was not part of the deal," she protested.

"I'm not really interested in the deal you made with my aunt. As far as I'm concerned, we both have a job to do, so put on the helmet and get on the bike."

Maggie stared at him uncertainly, suddenly aware that the valet and bellhop had stopped talking to watch her. Meeting Jake in front of the hotel had been a stupid idea. It wouldn't take more than a minute after her departure for everyone on staff to know she had gone off on the back of a motorcycle with a very shady character.

"Move it, honey."

Still Maggie hesitated. There was nothing teasing about Jake's manner this morning, and as her gaze traveled down to the bandage on his wrist, she felt a stab of remorse. Maybe he was in pain. Not that someone as macho as he would ever admit to such a simple human emotion. With a weary sigh, she turned the helmet around in her hand, trying to figure out how to put it on.

"I think this is too big," she said. "Is this for a woman?"

"It's for a passenger, male or female. I'm sorry I don't have a selection of colors to match your outfit, but I wasn't really planning on taking you along. In fact, I don't know why I'm doing it now. You'll probably jinx the trip and we'll wind up with a flat tire on some dead-end road in the middle of nowhere."

"That's a pleasant thought," she snapped. "And for your information, I wasn't planning on going along, either. But there's no reason for either one of us to be sarcastic, or this is going to be a terrible day. Now, tell me how to snap this thing on, so we can go, before I remember that I hate motorcycles."

Jake looked at her for a long moment. "Why do you hate bikes?"

"Because they make you vulnerable, at the mercy of others."

Jake shook his head. "They make you free. There's nothing like the feeling of the wind rushing past your face, the sun on your back. It's incredible. You feel the earth around you. You're not sitting in an air-conditioned limo listening to light rock on a top-forty station. You're battling nature."

"I think I'd rather be in a limo."

"Believe me, once you get on you won't."

She looked at him thoughtfully. "Why should I believe you? Have you ever ridden in one?"

"More times than I can count. Now, are you going to get on or what?"

"When were you in a limo?"

"You're stalling."

Maggie frowned and took a step forward. The machine looked big and solid. Jake looked as if he knew how to drive it, but then she remembered the holes in her garden and hesitated. "Are you sure about this?"

"What's the problem?"

"I don't know if I can trust you, even if you are Mrs. Castleton's nephew."

"Then just say goodbye. We don't have to do this."

"That's a tempting thought."

Jake shook his head before his mouth started to crack a smile. Finally, a chuckle came out, low and inviting, warming her soul, easing some of her doubts. "Come on, Maggie. You're not a coward, and I'm sure if I get out of line, you can deck me again." He slipped off his sunglasses so he could look her directly in the eye. "By the way, where exactly does your father, the marine colonel, live?"

"Texas, along with my oldest brother, Steve. Mike is in Kansas City and Jeff is in Germany. They're all in the service, so they move around a lot."

"But there's no one here in Napa?"

"No, but I can take care of myself."

"Right." He looked at her for a long moment, his eyebrows drawn up quizzically. "You know...I can't figure you out. The first time I saw you, I would have had you pegged for a straitlaced, uptight woman with serious ambition."

"And now?"

"Now, I know you talk to zucchini plants."

"Only Henry."

"And even though you don't like motorcycles, you're actually going to consider hopping on the back of my bike in a skirt so short it's going to stop traffic."

Maggie looked down at her white skirt, feeling inordinately pleased by the compliment. "I don't think anyone will crash from one look."

"You might be surprised."

His low muttered words brought her gaze back to his, and she couldn't look away. Something passed between them, strong and tantalizing and a little bit wild. It was ridiculous. She didn't even like him most of the time.

"What's it going to be, sweetheart? A walk on the wild side or a safe day at home?"

His words mirrored her thoughts, and she stroked the smooth sheen of the helmet with her fingers. "I should go home."

"Do you always do what you should do?"

"Most of the time. I was brought up to follow orders without question."

"Then get on the bike, dammit."

His smile took the edge out of his words, and she smiled back. "But as I've gotten older, I've learned to make my own decisions."

"Get on the bike, Maggie. Wrap your arms around my waist, and we'll ride like the wind. You know you want to."

Maggie sucked in a quick breath at the look in his eyes. He was more dangerous than the motorcycle. He was also a lot more exciting, and for a woman who had spent her whole life constricted by rules, his rebellious attitude was incredibly appealing. Maybe just once she'd go for broke.

Before she could change her mind, she put on her helmet, hitched up her skirt and swung her leg over the seat. Jake turned his head as she got comfortable and placed one hand on her bare thigh. "Slide in a little closer, honey. When we ride this bike, we ride as one."

Maggie swallowed hard and moved closer until her thighs met his. The rough edge of his jeans ground against her bare skin, creating all sorts of unwelcome erotic thoughts in her mind. This was crazy. This was foolish. It wasn't part of her plan.

"Now wrap your arms around me and hang on," Jake said, pulling her hands in front of his stomach, so tightly she could feel the clench of his abdominal muscles through his T-shirt. "Relax. Let yourself go with the bike. Feel the power. You're going to love this. You'll never be the same. Once you get a taste, you're going to want more."

That was exactly what she was afraid of.

Chapter Four

Although a surge of fear filled her as the powerful engine roared to life, Maggie clenched her jaw, closed her eyes and prayed to God that they'd at least make it out of the hotel parking lot before they hit anything.

As the motorcycle picked up speed and the air brushed against her face, she opened one eye and then the other, careful not to loosen her death grip on Jake's waist. As soon as she saw another car coming alongside them, she closed her eyes again, realizing that the only thing between her and the hard ground was Jake's body, which was something else she didn't want to think about.

Lord, she felt absolutely decadent, riding on the back of a Harley-Davidson in a miniskirt with a man who seemed to think he was the reincarnation of James Dean.

They pulled up to a traffic light and Jake set one foot on the ground to stabilize the bike. He turned his head to the side, a smile lurking around the corner of his mouth.

"Okay, honey?"

"Fine. Just fine," she lied.

"Where are we going?"

"I don't know. There are hundreds of wineries. We can go north, start at Yountville, then head into St. Helena and Calistoga."

"Whatever you want, Maggie. You're the tour guide."

"There's a small family winery a few miles north of here that makes champagne. We can start there."

"A woman who likes champagne. I should have guessed."

"Actually, I prefer a good cold beer on a hot day to just about anything else."

"Now you're talking. Maybe we should blow off this idea and find a nice cool pub somewhere."

"But your aunt wants you to buy some wine for the hotel."

Jake sighed. "Right, I forgot." He started to say something, but then the light turned green, and they were on their way again.

Gradually, as the traffic began to thin, and the highway became less traveled, Maggie started to relax and to her surprise began to enjoy the new sensations: the breeze against her face, the sun beating down on her back and shoulders, the gentle sway of the bike beneath her legs, the hard, muscled man in her arms.

Jake felt good, too good. She could not let herself get caught up in her reluctant attraction to him. He was not for her. She wanted roots, a place to call home and eventually marriage, the white picket fence, 2.5 children and a dog. Jake Hollister simply didn't fit the picture.

He was a handful—and what a handful. Maybe she'd just sit back and enjoy the moment. It was a beautiful day. In the distance were the mountains that separated Napa from its sister wine valley, Sonoma. Everything was green and lush. The flowers were blooming. The sky had only occasional wisps of clouds to mar its royal blue hue. And she felt a sense of belonging. This was her land, her home now. She had made a good choice.

Jake drove the bike along the Silverado Trail, the back way from Napa to Yountville. All along the road there were acres of grapes ripening for the upcoming harvest, the landscape occasionally broken up by a building or a barn, sometimes a stray horse or cow. They had been driving about fifteen minutes when Maggie saw the turnoff for the DeGavin Winery.

She tapped Jake on the shoulder and motioned for him to pull off the highway into the parking lot. This winery wasn't as luxurious as some of the others. There was a ranch-style house next to a barnlike building where the offices and cellars were housed, a swing set in the yard and a dog that barked eagerly at every new arrival.

Jake cut the engine and pulled off his helmet. He started to get off, but Maggie's arms were wrapped around his waist, a sensation she had gotten very used to.

"You can let go of me now," he said, slanting a look in her direction.

Maggie started at his words and then slowly peeled her fingers off his T-shirt. "Sorry."

"No problem. It might be easier if you got off first, although I won't have as nice a view."

"Right." Maggie tried to hold down her skirt as she swung one leg around the back of the bike and eased herself to the ground. She fiddled with the neck strap on her helmet.

After a moment, he took pity on her and reached up to unhook her helmet. His fingers brushed against her chin and the side of her neck. The look that passed between them was as potent as a glass of bubbly; if she wasn't careful, she was going to get drunk on Jake.

Turning away, she directed her attention to the winery, hoping that by the time he looked at her again, the color would have faded from her face.

"What did you think of the ride?" Jake put a hand on her shoulder, turning her to face him. "Not bad, huh?"

"No, it wasn't bad," she said, deliberately understating the joy she had felt.

He grinned at her. "Good. Then we can take it a little faster on the way back. You'll really be able to feel the speed, the power. It's incredible."

"Doesn't sound too safe."

"But it's fun."

Maggie looked at him thoughtfully. "And is that it for you? Fun? Is that all you want out of life?"

Jake nudged her toward the winery. "I think I need a couple of drinks before I handle a question like that." He paused. "Do you want to take the tour or go straight to the wine-tasting, or in this case, champagne-tasting?"

"Let's go get a drink," Maggie replied with a grin. "I'm thirsty."

Jake laughed. "A woman after my heart."

"No, I'm after champagne, not your heart."

His smile faded. "Good decision. That particular organ doesn't work too well for me anymore." With that, he walked over to the winery entrance and waited for her to catch up.

When they walked inside the main entry, Maggie found it much cooler there than the outside, which helped to dampen the heat that seemed to continually blaze between them. After looking at some of the historical information on the counters and on the walls, they made their way into the central tasting room and joined another group of tourists.

Jake squeezed his way up to the bar area and managed to get them each a glass of champagne. He handed one to Maggie and clinked his glass against hers.

"Down the hatch," he said.

"That's hardly an appropriate toast. How about 'here's to a nice day,' " she murmured, looking around to see if anyone had overheard him. But everyone else was listening to the wine maker talking about the techniques of bottling champagne.

Jake raised his glass and said, "Here's to no problems, no surprises and no more self-defense moves."

Maggie rolled her eyes. "I'll drink to the first two, but I'm saving the self-defense just in case I need it."

Jake laughed, took a sip of champagne and puckered his lips. "Very dry," he said.

Maggie followed suit and closed her eyes as the liquid slid down her throat. It was cool and tingly like a warm summer shower. "Nice," she said, opening her eyes to smile at him.

"Down the hatch." Jake raised his glass and drained the rest of the champagne in one long gulp. "Your turn."

"You're supposed to taste the stuff, not throw it back like a shot of tequila," Maggie said.

"We've got dozens of wineries to cover before the end of the day. And Aunt Ida already has tons of this stuff. I need to find her something a little more unusual."

Maggie shrugged. "Okay, fine." A half a glass of champagne certainly wouldn't hurt her. "But if we keep this up, we'll have to take a cab to each place."

"Don't worry. That was my first and last glass. You can do the rest of the tasting, and if you find something really special, I'll give it a try."

"But I don't know Mrs. Castleton's tastes."

"She'll like anything you do. And if she doesn't, maybe it will teach her not to do any more match-making."

"I'll drink to that," Maggie murmured as she followed Jake out to the motorcycle.

Two hours later, Maggie was feeling a lot more re-laxed as they walked out to the motorcycle. While she sat down on the back of the bike, Jake pulled out a map to study their course.

"One more winery on this stretch of highway, and we're done with this lot," he commented. "How are you holding up?"

"I feel good," Maggie said, with a small hiccup ac-companying her words.

Jake looked at her and started to chuckle. Her dark brown hair had come loose from her clips, billowing around her face in a soft cloud. Her blue eyes were lit up like a Christmas tree, and her cheeks were flushed a rosy pink.

"You're drunk," he said.

She shook her head, frowning at him like a prickly schoolmarm. "I couldn't possibly be drunk. I only drank this much at each place," she said, holding her fingers about an inch apart.

"I think those little tastes are beginning to add up."

Maggie smiled. "I'm fine, Jake, really. I can make one more place. But this time, you do the taste test."

"Deal."

He got back on the motorcycle and adjusted his helmet. Maggie slid her arms around his waist in preparation for their ride. He felt good, even better than before. Her fingers curled around the cloth of his T-shirt, and when he stretched his arms up to fasten his helmet, her fingers slid under the loose material and touched the firm muscles of his stomach.

Jake tensed and pulled her hands out from under his shirt. "Not a good idea, honey. Not while I'm trying to drive."

"Mmm. Are you sure?" she asked, resting her head against the back of his shoulder.

"You are drunk, aren't you?"

"No. Just relaxed."

"Great. I had to get you relaxed on the back of my motorcycle in the middle of a busy highway, where I can do absolutely nothing about it."

"What would you do?" she asked somewhat dreamily. "Kiss me again?"

"Among other things."

He turned the key in the ignition and pulled back onto the highway, fighting off a desire to turn around and take her home before his conscience had a chance to catch up. But he'd never taken advantage of a woman before, and he wouldn't start now, even if the curling of her fingers in the middle of his abdomen was making his jeans extremely uncomfortable.

Thankfully, the next winery was only a few minutes down the road, and this time when Jake got off the bike, he let out a deep sigh of relief. Distance. He needed a little bit of distance, not to mention a cold shower.

Maggie got off the bike more slowly and looked at him with a smile so lovely he wanted to kiss it right off her lips. Instead, he jerked his head toward the hill in front of them. "This is it."

Maggie looked around. "I've never been here before, but I've heard of it. It's unusual because you have to take a tram or a gondola or whatever they call it to the top of the hill. The winery is up on the ridge."

Jake looked at the glass-encased tram waiting at the foot of the hill and at the wire that would take them to the top. It looked like fun, almost like riding on a ski lift, but there wasn't any snow.

"I'm game," he said, reaching out to take Maggie's hand, but she resisted. When he paused to look at her, he realized her smile had glazed over and there was a spark of uncertainty in her eyes. "It's perfectly safe," he said, reading her mind.

Maggie shifted uncomfortably. "I'm sure it is. I just hadn't realized how high up the mountain it went."

"Mountain? This is a hill, honey, not the Swiss Alps. It shouldn't take more than ten minutes to get to the top. We'll be fine."

"Maybe you should go on your own. I've had enough to drink as it is."

"Which is exactly why I am not going to leave you down here all alone. Lord knows what kind of trouble you'd get into."

"I'll just wait by the bike. I'll keep an eye on it."

"You'll come with me. I'll hold your hand. You can close your eyes and pretend you're riding in an elevator."

"I don't know, Jake."

"Come on. You just rode on the back of a motorcycle. Today must be your day for trying new things. A walk on the wild side, remember?"

"Okay. Okay. Get me on that thing before I change my mind," she said, walking quickly over to the ticket booth.

There was a tram waiting in the station, and after getting their tickets, they boarded, and sat down on the bench seat along one side. There was ample room for at least five or six other people, but no one showed up, and after a few minutes, the station manager closed the tram door and with a creak and a groan it began its ascent to the top of the hill.

At the first jerky motion, Maggie slid a little closer to Jake, treasuring his large, reassuring body. When he put his arm around her shoulders, she welcomed the touch. In a way, she was surprised by his sensitivity. He might be a biker, a man with an attitude, but he also seemed to be a caring person, someone who understood fear but had the guts to face it head-on.

"I wish I had a little of your courage," she said, voicing some of her thoughts. "You don't seem scared of anything."

He looked straight ahead as he answered her. "Everyone is scared of something, but heights don't bother me."

"What scares you?" she asked.

He smiled to himself. "Neckties. Especially the ones with stripes. Turtleneck sweaters come a close second."

"Yeah, right."

"It's true. Every time I put either one on, I feel like I'm going to suffocate."

"Maybe you should get over it. Although you could probably avoid wearing turtleneck sweaters, sometimes neckties are essential to the job."

"Not any job in my future."

"I'm disappointed in you, Jake," Maggie said with a shake of her head. "I thought you were this brave, macho guy. But if a little necktie is going to do you in..."

"Hey, I was sharing a deep dark secret with you, and now you're making fun of me," he protested, throwing up his hands in exasperation. "Women. First they say you don't talk. Then when you do talk, they say you're ridiculous. You can't win. Why ask the question if you don't want to listen to the answer?"

Maggie looked at him in surprise. "I thought you were just putting me on."

Jake relented slightly. "Maybe a little. But I do have an aversion to ties."

"Neckties or all ties?"

"Very good, Miss Gordon. You get an A-plus for perception."

"Who was tying you down, Jake? Your ex-wife? The one who liked to reheat pies?"

"To name one," he said. "Look, let's just change the subject. We're taking a wonderfully slow ride up a hillside covered in grapes. The day is gorgeous. I just want to sit back and enjoy the view."

Maggie nodded, settling back against her seat. "Okay. At least you took my mind off this ride for a few minutes." Her gaze drifted to the view below them. It was green, peaceful. A haven. A little bit of paradise, her paradise. "This really isn't too bad," she said after a moment. "As long as I don't look up at that slim wire holding us, I think I'll be okay."

As if on cue, the tram came to a jerking stop, metal grating against metal in a frightening screech. Maggie uttered a small yell as she was thrown into Jake's arms. For a moment every nerve in her body screamed in anticipation of a hurtling descent to the hillside below them. The glass would shatter into a thousand pieces along with her body. Oh, God, she was too young to die. She hadn't bought her house. She hadn't met Mr. Right. She hadn't had kids. She hadn't made love to Jake.

My God, where had that thought come from? She didn't want to make love to Jake. She barely knew the man. Shaking that thought out of her mind, Maggie realized that they hadn't crashed at all. Instead, the tram was swinging back and forth in the air, and she was wrapped safely in Jake's arms.

His lips touched the top of her head as his arms tightened around her. "Easy, honey. We're okay."

Maggie's face was buried against his chest, and she was suddenly very aware of the warm, musk scent of his body, the beating of his heart beneath her cheek, the rise and fall of his chest as he breathed out the husky reassurance.

She knew she should move, straighten herself up and let him know that she didn't need anyone but herself to lean on. But it felt so good. And it got better.

Jake ran a hand through her hair, reaching under the heavy strands to cup the back of her neck. Then his fingers slid around to her shoulders, working on the knots of tension in her muscles. The massage wasn't particularly intimate, but where his fingers left off, her imagination took over, and she began to see the two of them doing a more thorough study of each other's bodies, but not in a tram swinging fifty feet above the ground, which at the moment wasn't moving.

With that thought in mind, Maggie moved her head, just enough so that she could judge the situation for herself. They weren't plummeting to the ground, but they also weren't continuing up the hillside.

"What happened?" she asked, looking into his twinkling green eyes.

"You threw yourself into my arms, again. Tell me, did you play tackle football as a child?"

"With three brothers? Of course."

"I should have figured."

Maggie moved a little farther out of his embrace but stayed close enough to hold on to him if she had to. If she was going to die, she wasn't going to worry about independence on the way down.

"Why are we stopped?" she asked again.

Jake shrugged. "I don't know. I'm not exactly an expert on tram rides. But I'm sure we'll get started again in a few minutes. There's nothing to worry about."

Maggie craned her head so she could see out each side of the tram. Unfortunately, there were several tall trees blocking her view of the bottom station, and although she saw another tram swinging a short distance below, there didn't appear to be any people on it. The station, apparently just over the ridge, at the top, was still obscured from view.

"I knew I shouldn't have gotten on this thing with you," she said with a sigh.

"Me? You're the one who's bad luck. I have the sore hand to prove it."

"You deserved that," she retorted. "And I'm not the one who walked in off the street and kissed a perfect stranger."

"That was definitely one of my better moments."

"By the way, who is Kathy?"

"Kathy?"

"The woman you mistook me for the other day."

"Oh, her, no one. I just made her up."

"But why?" She sat back on the bench seat and studied him. "Why would you do that?"

"It seemed like a good idea at the time. You looked so straight and uptight. I couldn't resist."

Maggie shook her finger at him. "You got me in trouble. Don't you think about the consequences of your actions?"

Jake's smile faded at her words. After a long pause, he shook his head. "You're right. I should have thought about it a little longer, but not for the reasons you think."

"What does that mean?"

"It means that I shouldn't have kissed you. It only made me want to do it again—and again."

Maggie looked away from him, not really sure how to react to his comment. It pleased her to know he was attracted. It also worried her. Because if he was feeling even half of what she was feeling, they were both in big trouble.

But nothing had to happen. Just because they admitted there was some chemistry between them didn't mean that they had to give in to it.

"I wish they'd get this thing going again. It's worse just sitting here, blowing in the wind," she said.

"Relax, Maggie. They're probably just loading some passengers. Haven't you ever been on a ski lift?"

"No. I'm not big on mountains. Sipping hot chocolate in the lodge is one thing but careening down a mountain path on three-inch pieces of wood is not my idea of fun."

"Always safe," Jake commented, running a finger along her jawline. "Risk-taking can be fun."

"Then I should be having fun right now."

He smiled. "I think I can arrange that." He lowered his head and kissed her.

It was a confident move, and he used her moment of surprise to gain complete access to her mouth, his tongue slipping into the warm cavern, setting off a surge of sensations that completely drove everything else from her mind. Just as he filled her mouth, he filled her senses.

She closed her eyes and kissed him back, sliding her arms around his neck, running her hands through his long curly dark hair, caressing the sides of his face and tugging gently at the gold earring in his ear. She wanted to touch every part of him, to know him as well as she knew herself.

"Oh, Maggie. Maggie," he murmured against her mouth. "You are so sweet."

She kissed the corner of his mouth. "I don't want to be sweet. I want to be sexy." The admission came from her heart, but she certainly hadn't meant to say it aloud. She stiffened in his arms and started to pull away.

"You are sexy," he said, looking directly into her eyes.

She swallowed hard. "We better stop."

"That would be the safe thing to do." He hesitated and then sighed and gently pushed her away from him. "You're right. This isn't going to work. I'm leaving in a few days. I spend my life on the road. And you—you're planting zucchini and baking apple pie. We don't exactly fit."

She nodded, knowing he was right, but feeling irritated with the entire situation. Her goals had seemed so clear before, but now they were getting increasingly hazy.

"Besides that," he continued, "you only kissed me because you're filled with wine and terrified you're going to die. By the time we get off, you'll be thanking your lucky stars you didn't let me..." His voice drifted away.

"Didn't let you what?"

Jake shook his head and remained silent, his jaw tight with tension, a pulse pounding away in his neck.

"Didn't let you what?" she repeated.

"Let it be. You're the one who wants to play it safe."

"I want to know."

"This." He reached over and unbuttoned the top two buttons of her blouse and slid his palm against her collarbone. "And this." He moved his hand lower to cup her breast in its lacy cup, his thumb sliding along the inside edge. "And this." He lowered his head and kissed her neck, trailing his mouth down the same line his hand had taken.

Maggie was trembling when he stopped to look at her, his eyes filled with questions, filled with desire.

"Tell me to stop," he said.

She stared at him for a long moment but didn't say a word.

"Tell me to stop, Maggie."

Chapter Five

Before Maggie could reply, the tram jerked into motion, catching her completely off guard. But this time, she grabbed on to the railing instead of Jake. When their ride seemed to be back to normal, she relaxed enough to look at Jake who had moved over to the other side of the tram and was staring out at the hillside with a somber expression on his face.

Part of her was sorry that they'd been interrupted, but another part of her was relieved. Things were happening much too fast. She had to get her bearings, think about what she was doing. But the silence was awkward and uncomfortable and she longed for the camaraderie that had developed between them over the past few hours.

"Timing is everything," she said as she rebuttoned her shirt. "Mine has always been lousy."

Jake looked at her and slowly smiled. She felt as if the sun had just come back out.

"Saved by the bell would probably be more appropriate," he said. He let another long pause go by and then he said, "Why the hell aren't you married?"

His question took her by surprise. "What—what do you mean?"

"I mean, why are you still loose, driving men crazy?"

"Do I really drive you crazy?"

"Oh, yeah. But answer the question."

She shrugged. "I almost got married once, a few years ago. Mark was in the military just like the rest of my family. They loved him."

"But you didn't?"

"I really tried to, Jake. I bought a dress, booked a banquet room, reserved the church...but I couldn't go through with it. When I spoke to Mark, he practically ordered me to go through with it. I realized then and there that I could never marry someone who didn't care about my feelings, about who I was. Of course, my dad was just as tough. Almost put a gun to my head. But in the end, he just threw up his hands and said, 'You know Maggie. She never does what she's supposed to do.'"

Jake nodded. "I'm impressed you didn't cave in under the pressure."

"I almost did, but I knew Mark wasn't for me. He would never have put my needs first. Never."

"I know what you mean," Jake said heavily, looking up as the tram neared the top of the hill. "Looks like we've finally arrived."

Maggie felt a keen sense of disappointment as they pulled into the tram station. She suddenly wished for more time alone, more time to talk, to share their pasts. But their moment was gone.

Maggie patted down her hair and checked the buttons on her blouse as the tram swung into the station.

A man grabbed the edge of their car and held it steady as she and Jake stepped out onto the ground.

"Sorry about the delay, folks. We had to load up some supplies at the bottom of the hill," he said.

"No problem," Jake replied. "It gave us a chance to..."

For one second Maggie thought he was going to tell the man exactly what they'd been doing. "Talk," she said hastily, jumping into the breach with a nervous laugh that denied her statement.

The man grinned knowingly. "Glad to hear it."

Maggie stalked away from the station, practically running up the steps toward the winery. She was embarrassed, humiliated and worst of all, she wished what hadn't happened had.

Jake yelled after her. "Wait up, Maggie."

She paused at the top of the steps and tapped her toe furiously. When he joined her, she snapped at him. "You are so annoying."

"What did I do now?"

"You practically told that man we were making love on the tram."

"I didn't say a word."

"It's what you *didn't* say."

"You were the one who laughed and turned red," Jake replied. "Give me a break."

"Ooh, I'd like to give you a break. I don't know why I came on this trip. It's been nothing but a disaster."

"We had a few good moments back there."

"I don't want to talk about that."

"Figures." He shook his head as if he couldn't figure her out. "Look, we're here. It took a lot for us to get here, why don't we just go inside and see what they have to offer?"

"Fine." Maggie headed for the entrance. "But you do the taste test. I've had enough craziness for one day."

"Whatever you want," he said.

The winery had a definite Spanish style to it, with cool red-patterned tiles on the floor, white stucco walls and dark wood frames along the doorways and windows. In the tasting room there was a long bar along one side and ceiling-to-floor windows on the other. An open door led out to a patio where circular tables topped with colorful umbrellas were set out for visitors to sit down and enjoy the view.

While Jake lined up at the bar, Maggie ventured over to the windows and finally stepped out to the patio to take another look at the valley in the afternoon sunshine. Everything was quiet and peaceful, nothing like the turbulent emotions running through her.

Jake was forcing her to think about things, to analyze her life, to rationalize her decisions, and she didn't like it. Who was he to come into her life and force his devil-may-care attitude on her? She had goals. She had dreams. She had house payments to make.

"Here you are," Jake said as he came up next to her. "I thought you might have ditched me."

"How would I have gotten home?"

He smiled at her practicality. "Good point. Why don't you try this wine? I think it's pretty good." He handed her a glass of chardonnay and watched as she took a sip. "What do you think?"

"It's good. But I'm not very discriminating when it comes to wine."

"What about men?" he asked.

Maggie drew in a breath and let it out, wondering why even the simplest conversation with Jake turned into a duel. "I'm very discriminating when it comes to men. I almost made one mistake. I won't get that close again unless I'm damn sure it's the right thing to do."

Jake stared at her for a long moment. "You sound like me. I took the plunge and almost drowned. I'm not sure I want to get into that swimming pool again."

"It is a big risk," she agreed.

"Now, what about the wine? Shall I buy a bottle for Aunt Ida?"

"Yes," Maggie replied. "At least she'll be happy we didn't come back empty-handed."

"As long as your hand is in mine, I think Aunt Ida will be thrilled with our day's work," Jake said with a grin, taking the glass out of her hand.

Maggie shook her head in confusion. "I don't get it, Jake. Why is your aunt so determined to see us together?"

"She likes you."

"I appreciate that. I like her, too. But that doesn't explain her matching up you and me. Anyone can see just by looking at us that we are totally different."

Jake tugged at her collar that was now firmly buttoned up as high as it would go. "Just because you dress more conservatively than I do doesn't mean you aren't a rebel at heart."

"But I'm not a rebel," she protested, stepping back from his wandering hand. "Far from it. I was brought up to respect God, my parents and the U.S. Marine Corps. I go to church on Sunday. I pay my taxes. I work nine to five and sometimes more without punching in for overtime. I never park in a loading zone, and I always stop when the light turns yellow."

Jake burst out laughing. "But you're willing to ride on the back of my bike, and you talk to vegetables. I think there's a rebel inside you dying to get out."

Maggie sighed and turned away from him, resting her arms on the wall that surrounded the patio. "Sometimes I don't know who I am. My father thinks I'm a rebel because I want a home, and I don't want to be in the Marine Corps. I don't want to line up and salute him like a good little soldier. My family doesn't understand me. They thinks I'm nuts."

"You're not crazy. You just march to your own beat. Like I do. What do you care what they think, anyway? You're a grown woman. Live your own life."

"I'm trying. Believe me, I'm trying. But sometimes I feel guilty for turning my back on them. They're my family."

"You didn't disown them, Maggie. You just chose your own way to live. There's nothing wrong with that." Jake's words rang out with deep conviction.

"You sound like you understand, Jake. But how could you? I can't see you trying to fit into anyone's uniform."

"Yeah, well, I haven't always been this smart. Come on, let's go buy a bottle of wine and hit the road."

Maggie hesitated, wanting to pursue the conversation but sensing that Jake would only tell her as much as he wanted to. Who was this man Jake Hollister, anyway? For some reason, she didn't think there was a simple answer to that question. He was a very private man, and that wasn't going to change unless he wanted it to. He was a complicated man, but someone with heart, someone that understood.

He was getting under her skin. And it wasn't just the flirting, the sexy come-on smile or the way he kissed, but everything else, the things he didn't say, and the edge of pain in his voice when he mentioned the past.

She knew that there had to be more behind his choice of a carefree life-style than just the lack of something better to do. He knew too much about things. He was obviously well educated, and Mrs. Castleton had implied that he knew a great deal about the hotel business—meaning what? Another question she couldn't answer.

With an annoyed shake of her head, Maggie decided to stop trying to figure him out. It was probably better if she didn't know any more about him. Then, she could try to keep her distance. Yeah, right.

"Maggie," Jake called to her from inside the room, two bottles of wine in his hand. "Tram's leaving in one minute."

"Coming." She took one last look at the valley below, her land, her home. It was something to focus on, something she could remember on the way back to the hotel when she was riding pillion, her arms wrapped around Jake's waist, her thighs touching his.

"Maggie. We're losing daylight."

That wasn't all she was losing, Maggie thought as she walked over to join him.

Fortunately, the tram was filled on the trip down, and she and Jake didn't have to talk. There were no delays, and they were down at the bottom of the hill before they knew it. The bike was waiting where they had left it, and Maggie donned her helmet while Jake stashed the bottles of wine in the storage compartment.

As she slid onto the bike, Maggie moved to the very back edge. Touching him again seemed an almost overwhelming idea. She was afraid of the feelings he evoked in her, terrified that she wouldn't be able to stop the intense physical desire that she felt for him. It had never been this way for her before. Men had never aroused more than a passing curiosity, not even her ex-fiancé. Mark had kissed her, lots of times, but never in such a hungry way, as if he would starve without her.

She cleared her throat and adjusted her helmet. She had to stop her imagination. It was way out of control. Flirting with Jake was not going to get her anywhere. He had candidly admitted that the last thing he wanted was a home or ties of any kind.

Oh, he'd probably be happy to have a fling, but then he'd leave, and she'd be alone. Maybe she could handle it, she thought in desperation, a quick affair just to get him out of her system. But she had never been the type. Her emotions always got caught up in what her body was doing. She couldn't separate having sex from making love, and she didn't really want to.

"Are you ready, Maggie?" Jake asked as he got on the motorcyle.

"As ready as I'll ever be."

"You're not still scared of this thing, are you?"

"I'd feel more comfortable in a car, but I'm getting used to this."

Jake turned his head so he could see her face. "Stop fighting so hard, Maggie."

"Fighting what?" she asked warily, wondering if he could really read her that easily.

"Yourself. Your own true nature. Just be who you are and let everyone else work around that. Now, hold on tight, because I'm going to kick up some dust on our way back, let you feel the power of this baby."

Maggie wrapped her arms around his body and felt the power. Boy, did she feel the power. And the motorcycle wasn't even moving yet.

Thirty minutes later, Jake turned off the highway and began weaving his way through the neighborhood around the hotel. There was a main suburban plaza on one side of the block, boasting everything from groceries to videos in a one-stop shopping sprawl of small businesses. The next block was more old-fashioned with antique stores and various clothing shops along a main street bordered with trees and flowers.

Instead of continuing to the hotel, which was still a couple of blocks away, Jake pulled into a parking spot on the street and cut the engine.

"What are you doing?" Maggie asked. "I thought we were going back."

"I'm hungry."

"There's a restaurant at the hotel."

"I know, but there's ice cream here." Jake tilted his head toward Schaeffer's Ice-Cream Parlor and Candy Shop. "You do like ice cream, don't you?"

Maggie rolled her eyes. "Are you kidding? It's my number-one vice."

His eyes twinkled at her choice of words. "Definitely sinful. What do you say? Shall we sin together?"

"You *are* still talking about ice cream, aren't you?"

"Of course," he said, his eyes flashing with mischief.

Maggie slid off the bike. Maybe it was a good idea to stop for a few minutes. They could end their day on a better note and face Mrs. Castleton together. Besides that, ice cream always had a way of making her feel better.

Jake led the way into the old-fashioned ice-cream parlor and Maggie followed him with a smile. His biker looks seemed out of place in a shop with chocolate truffles, pinwheel suckers and red and black licorice. Another contradiction in his tough guy character.

As they stepped up to the ice-cream counter, Jake pulled his wallet out of his jeans. "My treat, honey. So go ahead and splurge."

The man behind the counter was in his early forties with thinning brown hair and an engaging pair of dark eyes. Maggie knew that Pete had wanted to own an ice-cream store since he was a little kid, and she could definitely understand why. There was something about the stuff that made her go crazy.

"You're telling her that, Jake? She's one of my best customers," Pete said. "Let me tell you, she can put it away."

"That's supposed to be our little secret," Maggie said, pausing as she stopped to consider the rest of his sentence. "And how do you know his name? He's only been in town two days."

"I stopped in yesterday," Jake explained.

"And the day before," Pete added. "If he stays in town, I may be able to give Lily a raise."

The short blond woman scooping ice cream at the other end of the counter laughed at that comment. "That'll be the day. Don't get married, Maggie. It pays slave wages."

"But there are fringe benefits," Pete said, exchanging a warm, teasing smile with his wife.

Maggie watched the exchange with a sudden longing in her breast. Pete and Lily were so obviously in love, so in tune with each other that she couldn't help but feel envious. How wonderful it would be to find a partner, someone to love with, to live with, to share a life with. Someone to fit into her life, not the other way around.

"How long are you going to be in town, Jake?" Pete asked, breaking into her thoughts. "So I can plan my ice cream ordering."

"A few days. Then I'll be moving on."

"Moving on where?"

"Yes, where?" Maggie echoed with genuine interest.

Jake shrugged. "Don't know yet. Wherever the mood strikes me."

"Must be nice to be that free," Pete said. "You two think about what you want. I'm going to help these ladies, if you don't mind."

Maggie shook her head and stepped back so the older women behind her could place their order.

"What are you going to have?" Jake asked.

Maggie stared up at the menu on the wall. "I'm not sure. Maybe a shake or a sundae."

"A shake? You can do better than that. How about Angel's Delight? That sounds just like you, vanilla ice cream topped with coconut. Pure and heavenly."

Maggie shot him a warning look as one of the ladies in front of them turned around and smiled.

"Or maybe Fudge Fantasy for some nice chocolate decadence," Jake continued. "Oh, wait. Look at that. Sassy Sundae. They must have named that after you."

"Jake, please. I'm trying to think."

"And I'm trying to help."

"You're distracting me," she murmured.

Jake leaned over to her. "You're doing a lot worse to me."

She shot him a warning look, but he ignored her.

"In fact, I think I know the solution to our problem. Let's go all the way. Let's do it. Afternoon Delight, baby."

The woman in front of them gasped. "Oh, my."

"He's talking about ice cream," Maggie said sharply, masking the shivery feeling that had shot through her at his words.

"You mean she thinks...?" Jake looked at the woman with an appropriately shocked expression. "My goodness. What is this world coming to?"

"Excuse me." The woman brushed past them with a red face to match her strawberry ice cream.

"You're terrible," Maggie said with a helpless shake of her head. "And you enjoyed that."

"It was probably the most excitement she's had all week." He lowered his head, smiled sexily and whispered in her ear. "How do you know I was only talking about ice cream?"

Maggie swallowed hard, an immediate picture forming in her mind of sunshine swamping her bed in the middle of the afternoon and Jake lying back on the pillows, the light gilding his beautiful naked body.

"What it will be, folks?" Pete asked.

"Huh?" Maggie asked in confusion as both men turned to her with an inquisitive eye. "Oh, ice cream."

"That's what we're here for," Jake said with another sexy grin.

"I'd like Angel's Delight," she decided. Maybe it would help her focus on purity of thought.

"I'll take Devil's Choice," Jake said. "They seem to go together."

"About as well as we do," she replied.

"Hey, we both like ice cream. It's a start."

"And an end. When we go back to the hotel, I want to see your aunt."

"So you can tell her what a wonderful day you had?"

"No, so I can tell her she should find someone else to baby-sit you."

"But we're having so much fun."

Maggie shook her head, took her ice-cream dish off the counter and walked over to a table. A few moments later, Jake joined her and for a while they were content to simply focus on their ice cream. When her dish was empty, Maggie sat back with a satisfied smile. At least one hole in her stomach had been filled.

"Feeling better?" Jake asked.

"Much. Thanks."

"You're welcome."

Maggie folded her arms on the table and stared at Jake, wondering if she should leave things alone or give in to her curiosity.

"Okay, what do you want to know?" Jake asked, reading her expression so clearly it was scary.

"Where are you going when you leave here? Back to your apartment in L.A., or somewhere else?"

"I really don't know yet."

"But how can you not know where you're going to be in a few days? Don't you have to make plans?"

"Making plans isn't part of my vocabulary anymore."

"But it was at one time?"

"Why are you so curious about me?"

She shrugged, realizing her interest in him was out of all proportion to the brief amount of time they had spent together. "No reason. I just can't figure you out."

"That makes two of us. You're a complete mystery to me, too."

Maggie smiled, feeling somewhat pleased by the comment. Being a woman of mystery was a lot better than being dull and boring. "Sometimes I'm a mystery to myself," she said. "I set goals and I aim straight toward them, but somewhere along the way I seem to get sidetracked, usually by people or things that are bad for me."

"Maybe your goals just aren't right for you."

"This time they are. This time I know what I want."

"The house."

"No, not just a house—a *home.* I want to be like my mother. She was the perfect homemaker. She could make a gourmet meal out of chili beans. My father adored her."

"What happened to your mom?"

Maggie looked down at the table and dabbed her finger at a drop of ice cream. "She died when I was a kid."

"I'm sorry. It must have been rough for you." Jake shook his head. "But don't you see the futility, Maggie? You aim for something and find out when you get there that it's either gone or nothing like what you expected. In my opinion, you just have to live each day, take what you get and try to enjoy it."

"And that makes you happy? Really happy? Not knowing what's around the next corner?"

"Yes. It's exciting. It's an adventure. If you know the end of a book, what's the point in reading it?"

"I don't know," she said in confusion, caught up in his creative approach to life, drawn to it more than she wanted to be. "We should go. I want to talk to your aunt. And I have things I need to do at home."

Jake stood up. "I forgot. Your house comes first."

"I'm sure you have other things to do, as well," Maggie said, getting to her feet. "Aren't you supposed to be spying on the hotel employees?"

"Who told you that?"

"Mrs. Castleton said you were going to give her some advice on the hotel. She implied that you're quite ex-

perienced in such matters.'' Maggie sent him a
thoughtful look. "Sounds like you must have had some
sort of job in your life."

Jake smiled grimly. "I think you're right, Maggie.
It's time to have a little chat with Aunt Ida."

Chapter Six

By the time they got back to the hotel, Maggie was determined to end her association with Jake Hollister. She waited politely while he parked the bike. Even when he handed her a bottle of wine to carry inside, she didn't say a word. She had said too much already, telling him things about herself that she normally reserved for very close friends.

No, it was time to break things off. She would simply tell Mrs. Castleton that she was going to be very busy for the next few days and that someone else would have to show Jake around. If that put a black mark on her record, so be it. At least her heart would stay intact.

"Do you want to go straight up to my aunt's suite?" Jake asked as they walked into the hotel.

Maggie didn't hear his question, she was too caught up in rehearsing what she was going to say to Mrs. Castleton. She also didn't notice the surprised look on the bellboy's face or the man standing in the lobby talking to one of the guests. It wasn't until she heard her name called out in sharp, accusing tones, that she paused and looked around.

"Miss Gordon," Harry Stone repeated as he ended his conversation with an elderly woman and walked over to her. "You're not due to go on duty for another hour. What are you doing here?"

Maggie looked at him in confusion, suddenly realizing that her hair was completely windblown from the ride, and she was holding a bottle of wine in her hand, not to mention the fact that Jake's arm had moved around her shoulders at some point during their entrance into the hotel.

Quickly, she stepped away, looking at Jake and then at Mr. Stone, wondering how on earth she was going to explain her way out of this one. "I—I, uh—"

"I'd like to see you in my office," Harry interjected. "Immediately."

"We're kind of busy right now," Jake said, taking a step closer to her.

"Jake, I think I should go."

"But you don't go on duty for another hour."

"Yes, but—"

"Then what's the problem?"

As he asked the question, Jake directed his gaze toward Harry. The other man flinched but didn't back down. "Miss Gordon, if you value your job, please follow me into my office."

"Yes, sir."

"Maggie, you don't have to—"

"Yes, I do," she said, cutting him off this time. "I'll just be a minute. I'll meet you upstairs."

Jake looked as if he wanted to argue the point, but finally he nodded and walked away.

Maggie sighed and followed Harry into his office, exchanging a look of commiseration with the other desk clerk as she walked by.

As soon as she entered Harry's office, he closed the door behind her, pulling down the window shade so that their conversation would be completely private.

"What were you doing with that man?" he demanded without preamble.

"I showed him some of the wineries in the area," Maggie replied, wishing she could tell him that the trip had been solely at Mrs. Castleton's call, but she had given the woman her word.

"We have a rule, Miss Gordon. No fraternizing with the guests."

"Yes, sir."

"So you're aware of the rule?"

"I am now."

"That's not good enough. What is going on with you and this man? You said you didn't know him the other day and now I find you together again."

"There's nothing going on. And I didn't know him then. I barely know him now. It was an innocent outing."

"Innocent?" He laughed in disbelief. "Then why are you meeting him upstairs? Another innocent outing?"

Maggie's jaw dropped open at his insinuation. "I'm certainly not planning on doing what you're thinking. I was just carrying this upstairs for him," she said, holding out her bottle of wine.

"I don't really care what your plans are, because as of now, you're going to cancel them. Employees do not mingle with the guests. I assume you still want to be an employee?''

"Of course I do."

"Good. Because this is your final warning. The next time you break or bend one of our rules, you'll be terminated. Now, why don't you go home and get cleaned up before you go on duty." He paused and held out his hand. "I'll have one of the bellboys deliver that bottle of wine."

Maggie handed him the bottle, hesitating as his fingers circled the neck of the bottle. The moment turned tense, their struggle silent but clear, and then Maggie let go. She had no other choice.

Jake paced restlessly around his aunt's living room. Ida sat on the couch watching him, a bemused look on her face as he stopped to pick up a jade figurine and then set it back down without really looking at it. He had been waiting for Maggie to join him for more than twenty minutes. But she still hadn't appeared, and he had a bad feeling about the entire situation.

Walking over to the window, he slit the blinds with his fingers and peered out at the employee parking lot. Her orange Volkswagen was still parked at the far corner. And then he saw her.

Maggie was walking slowly, her head turned toward the ground, her shoulders hunched as if she had been beaten down. Obviously her meeting with her manager had not gone well. And it was his fault. He shouldn't have gone out with her.

Everything was getting messed up. His simple trip was turning into a nightmare of complications. He was supposed to do a job, not get caught up in a pair of beautiful blue eyes and a smile so warm and generous, he felt as if he could bask in its warmth forever.

Maggie Gordon was not for him. She would ask a lot from a man, and she deserved to get it. But not from him. He didn't have anything left to give.

"What are you staring at?" Ida queried impatiently. "You're making me very nervous."

"Maggie's going home," he replied, turning around to face her.

"Home? I thought she wanted to talk to me."

"That was before that jerk of a manager cornered her in the lobby. I don't think he liked seeing her with me."

"Oh, dear," Ida's mouth turned down into a frown. "This isn't going right at all."

"At last we agree." He walked toward the door. "I'm going to go downstairs and tell that idiot who he's dealing with."

Ida immediately shook her head. "You can't do that, Jake. Not yet."

"I'm not going to let Maggie take the heat for this. It isn't her fault."

"There's something I haven't told you."

Jake rolled his eyes and then slowly walked back toward the middle of the room, planting his fists on his hips. "God help me. What is it?"

"Sit down, Jake."

He sighed and did as he was told. "Okay, shoot."

"Someone has been stealing from the hotel. I'm very concerned that it might be Harry Stone."

"Embezzlement?" Jake looked at her in surprise. "Uncle Bill didn't say anything about embezzlement."

"He doesn't know. It's only a small amount of money, a few glitches in the books that anyone might chalk up to a mistake, but somehow I don't think that's what it is."

"What about your accountant?"

"He reports to Harry. And no one has said anything to me. They think I haven't noticed, but they think I don't read anything, that I just take their word for how things are going."

"Then they're bigger fools than I thought." Jake leaned back against the couch, kicking up one foot on the edge of the coffee table as he thought about her problem.

"That's why I wanted you to come down and check things out, Jake. Of course, it's not just the money. We've had a lot of employee turnover in the past few months and even the bookings are down. I don't understand it. We used to have such an excellent reputation, but somehow it's being whittled away, right out from under me. The last thing I want is for the family to think I failed. I have to get things back on track."

Jake nodded, giving her a smile of commiseration. He knew how tough and unforgiving the family could be when it came to mistakes with their business. "You told Maggie I was here to check out the hotel, didn't you?"

"Yes."

"Why? She could be part of the problem."

Ida shook her head. "I don't believe that for a second. You only have to know her a short while to realize she is completely honest—too honest, probably. The only flaw she seems to have is a soft spot for people that tends to make her a little less than efficient at times."

"Which is why Stone is always on her back?"

"He's on everyone's back," Ida replied. "I think he's nervous about the way things are going. Or maybe he's the culprit. I wish I knew. The man has been working for me for six years, but lately, he's changed. I don't feel I know him anymore.''

"Have you tried to talk to him?''

"I've tried, Jake. He simply won't open up. I hate to go behind his back, but at this moment I don't feel I have another choice.''

Jake ran a hand through his hair. "That may be true, but I wish you hadn't gotten Maggie involved. You put her in a tough spot.''

"Nothing's going to happen to Maggie. I won't let it. But for now, we need to keep Harry in the dark about your identity. Please, Jake, this is important.''

Jake stood up and stretched, knowing that Ida's stubbornness easily matched his own. "Fine. When can I see the books?''

"Tonight. At least my copy of the records. And on Thursday I'm taking Harry and the senior staff to dinner. Maggie will be working the front desk, and while the other clerk is on dinner break, you'll have free run of that area.''

"Except for Maggie.''

"Is that a problem, dear? Didn't you two have a nice day together?''

Jake smiled at her. "You have to stop matchmaking, Aunt Ida. It's not going to work. Maggie Gordon is not the woman for me.''

"But she's lovely.''

"I'm not talking about her looks.''

"Neither am I. She's nothing like Carole. She cares about more than money and material things. She has a heart.''

"But I don't, not anymore.''

Ida shook her head and poured herself a cup of tea from the silver tea service. "Suit yourself. I'm not going to do another thing to interfere. I just wanted you two to meet. The rest is up to you."

"I'm leaving in a couple of days."

"So you keep saying."

"Look, isn't there any way I can get into the office tonight?"

"Thursday is the perfect time. Besides, what's the rush? It's not like you have to be somewhere." She paused. "Or are you afraid if you stay too long, you won't want to leave?"

"No. I'm definitely leaving. And right now I'm going to my room. By the way…" Jake walked over to the table and picked up one of the bottles of wine he had bought for her. "Maybe you'd like to try this."

Ida took the bottle from his hand and read the label with a frown. "Oh, dear. Is this the best you could find?"

"No, but it's what you get for meddling in my life."

"I just want you to be happy," she said with a loving smile. "People weren't meant to live alone."

"You're alone."

"That's different. I'm older. I've had my share of love. My time is passed. You deserve to be happy."

"I am happy," he snapped.

"Are you really?"

He threw up his hands. "Why won't anyone believe me?"

"Maybe because you're lying to yourself. And you liked Maggie, didn't you? Tell the truth."

Jake walked out of the room and slammed the door on her question. But then he hesitated, feeling years of politeness training poking at his conscience. Aunt Ida was just trying to be nice. He raised his hand to knock at her door and then heard the music, soft and lilting, and her voice in accompaniment as she sang, "Isn't It Romantic."

His hand dropped to his side and he walked away. Romance was not for him. Aunt Ida would just have to accept that fact. The sooner the better.

The next morning, Maggie woke up with a headache. And its name was Jake. Thankfully, he had stayed out of her way the night before. She hadn't seen or heard from him during her evening on duty. Hopefully, it would stay that way for the rest of his stay.

He was like a hot fudge sundae, delicious and fattening, a special treat, not something to indulge in every day.

She struggled out of bed, wrestling with the covers that had twined around her body during a long, sleepless night. Then she stood up and stretched, stifling a yawn as she headed for the bathroom. A shower would revive her, a cold one.

Then she would get back to what was important in her life, her job, her house, her zucchini and her apple pie. Her mouth scrunched up at the thought. The darn pie was becoming the bane of her existence, and the county fair started on Friday, three days away. It was now or never.

After a quick shower, she threw on a pair of blue jeans and a sleeveless T-shirt and headed for the kitchen. She pulled out the familiar pieces of paper, the ones written by her grandmother, as well as her own typed transcript. There had to be a secret somewhere. She just didn't know where. She'd thought she was following the directions exactly.

While her mind worked on deciphering the perfect filling, her hands went to work on the familiar crust. At least she had mastered one part of the process. Making the dough had become almost second nature.

With that done, she wiped a floury hand across her forehead and read through the list of ingredients: apples, white sugar, brown sugar, raisins, lemon juice. How could she go wrong? But something wasn't quite right. Somewhere the measurements were slightly off keel. A pinch of this and a dab of that weren't very exact, especially to a cooking novice like herself.

Maybe she should just give up on the pie, or bake something from a standard recipe, but then it wouldn't be special. It wouldn't be hers. It wouldn't win. And Maggie was determined to win. Her mother had been a gourmet cook. She ought to be able to at least bake a pie.

With determination, she pulled out a bag of apples and started to peel them. Then the phone rang, and her body stiffened. It wasn't necessarily Jake. It could be any one of her friends or co-workers from the hotel. Still...

Irritated with herself, she dropped the knife and picked up the receiver. "Hello," she said sharply.

"Maggie, girl. Is that you?"

"Daddy?" Her voice changed from confident to unsure. "Hi, how are you?"

"Terrific. And I've got great news."

"What's that?"

"Mike is getting married. Found himself a beauty. Name's Lois. She's a marine, too. We've got another soldier in the family, honey."

"That's great," Maggie said halfheartedly. Not that she didn't feel happy for Mike, but the thought of another woman in the family was unsettling. She had been the only feminine influence for so long. Now there would be someone else, and she was a marine. Her lips turned down into a frown. Lois would probably feel more like one of the family than Maggie did.

"Maggie, did you hear me?" her father asked.

Maggie straightened, realizing she'd been daydreaming. "Sorry."

"I said, he's getting married in three weeks. We want you to come to Texas for the wedding."

"Texas?" Maggie asked, scrambling for something to say. Take off a couple of days and run down to Texas? Harry Stone would have a fit. Still, it was her brother. She should be there. But if she went home, the same old arguments would come up, and she wasn't sure she was ready to handle them yet. "I'd like to come," she said finally, "but I don't know if I can get the time off."

"Your brother's getting married, girl. You get yourself down here. If they don't like it at that job of yours, just pack your bags and come on home."

Maggie shook her head, feeling the familiar wave of frustration. "Texas isn't home to me, Dad. This is my home now."

"Your family's here."

His voice held more than a hint of impatience in it. But then, he wasn't used to anyone going against his wishes. After commanding the troops, ordering one rebellious daughter around was a piece of cake for him.

"For now," she said sharply. "But who knows where you'll be next year or the year after. I don't want to move around anymore. I want to stay put. I want to have a home. I want to make a pie."

He snorted so loudly she had to jerk the receiver away from her ear. "You burn toast, girl."

"I'm becoming a very good cook. Just like Mom."

"Your mom would have thought more of you if you'd married Mark. He would have taken good care of you," her dad said grumpily.

"I don't want to be taken care of. I can handle my own life, thank you," she replied, forcing herself not to be intimidated by him. "And we've been through this before, dozens of times. Why can't you just accept me for what I am?"

"Huh?"

Maggie sighed. "Forget it. Look, I'm happy for Mike, and I'll try to make it to the wedding. But I have to go now. I'll talk to you later."

She set the receiver down as soon as she heard his muttered goodbye. He was just as frustrated with her as she was with him. They had never clicked, never. He always wanted her to be one way and she wanted to be the other. Deep down, she knew that she kept hoping that if she was more like her mother, he would love her as much as he had loved her mother. But that wasn't going to happen. It just wasn't.

Blinking back an angry tear, she picked up a knife and whacked at the peel on an apple, venting her frustration on the innocent piece of fruit. But in her hurry, the blade slipped and caught her finger. She yelped in pain as bright drops of blood began to flow from the cut. Then she started to cry, not because of the injury, but because of her own mixed-up thoughts and years of feeling left out. She wanted her own home, her own family, someone to love.

Jake was just about to knock on Maggie's back door when he heard a clatter and a sharp cry. His body tightened with alarm and he shoved open the kitchen door, sending it flying against the wall.

Maggie looked at him with teary, stunned eyes, and he stared back at her with the same shock, the same intensity, the same longing. She looked like a wounded sparrow, her hair flying around her face, her blue eyes filled with hurt, her shoulders trembling. She looked smaller than before, standing there in bare feet, blue jeans and a T-shirt. An overwhelming surge of protectiveness filled him. He wanted to do battle, to hurt whatever had hurt her. But the wounded little bird suddenly turned into an outraged peacock.

"What the heck do you think you're doing barging in here like that?" she asked. "Haven't you heard of knocking?"

He took a step back in surprise. "I heard you yell. I thought someone was attacking you." His gaze dropped to her injured hand. "What happened?"

"I cut myself," she said, reaching for a napkin to soak up the blood. "It's nothing."

Jake watched her fumbling for a moment and then took a towel off the kitchen counter, soaked it in cold water and asked for her hand. It was probably a mistake, he thought, and when his fingers touched hers, he was sure it was.

The action brought them close together and Maggie's hair drifted across his cheek, the fragrant scent of shampoo sending his hormones into overdrive. She shifted her body, the soft womanly curve of her breast brushing against his arm. He bit down on his lip and fought back an urge to pull her into his arms. He hadn't wanted a woman this intensely in years.

Roughly, he took her good hand and placed it over her injured finger so that he could move away from her. "Do you have any bandages around here?"

"In the bathroom," she said quietly, meeting his gaze.

He saw confusion in her eyes—and desire. It almost undid him. If one of them didn't fight this crazy attraction, they were going to end up on the floor again, and this time she wouldn't have to flip him to get him there.

"Down the hall," she added when he didn't move.

He started at her voice. "Right. I'll get you one. Keep the pressure on that finger."

Jake strode down the hall, pausing as he passed the bedroom. An irresistible kick of curiosity drew him in. Her bed was unmade, deliciously rumpled from the curves of her body, and it looked as if she'd had a restless night. The peach-colored comforter was halfway off the bed, revealing floral sheets. There was a book on the nightstand and a bottle of aspirin. On the floor next to the bed was an empty pint of ice cream. He smiled at that, letting his gaze drift through the rest of the room, noting a shirt and some jeans tossed on a chair and a closet that revealed a mixture of neat shelves and slightly mussed clothing.

Everything about the room was appealing to him. It looked the way a home should—relaxed, lived in, comfortable, nothing like what he had grown up in or married into. This was a room where a man could kick off his boots and throw himself down on the bed, a nice king-size bed, he noted with appreciation. Plenty of room for two.

"Jake, where are you? I'm bleeding all over the floor," Maggie called out.

Jake jerked at the sound of her voice, feeling like an intruder, and hastily made his way into the bathroom. The medicine cabinet was directly over the sink and he opened it, hoping to find the bandages inside. What he found was the most organized cabinet he had seen in his life. Everything was labeled and placed in alphabetical order. He grinned and then started to chuckle. At least it was easy to locate the Band-Aids under B.

Taking the box out of the cabinet, he walked back to the kitchen. "Tell me, Maggie. Has your father been here?"

She looked at him in confusion. "Why do you ask?"

"Your medicine cabinet. It looks like something a marine colonel would set up."

"Habit," she said, making a face. "Some things stick with you no matter how hard you try to get rid of them."

"I know what you mean." He held out a bandage. "Here."

"Can you put it on my finger for me?" Maggie asked.

For some reason, touching her again, especially with the bedroom so clear in his mind, did not seem like a good idea. He had come to set things straight, not muck them up. But he could hardly abandon an injured woman.

With a grim look, he fastened the Band-Aid around her finger and backed up until his legs hit the counter. It was then he noticed the array of cooking utensils spread around the kitchen and the delightful streak of flour across her forehead. A reluctant smile curved his lips. "Not another pie? No wonder you're crying."

Maggie rubbed her eyes with the back of her hand. "It was the cut, that's all."

"Really? Is anything else wrong?"

"My brother's getting married, if you must know," she replied sharply.

He raised an eyebrow. "And that makes you cry? Why?"

"Do I have to have a reason? Can't I just cry if I want to?" she challenged.

He held up his hands in apology. "You can scream if you want to. Whatever makes you happy."

"I might try that next. What are you doing here, anyway?"

"You were supposed to talk to Aunt Ida with me. What happened?"

Maggie turned her back on him and walked over to the counter to resume peeling her apples. "I got called on the carpet. That's what happened. As if you didn't know."

"I'm sorry about that."

"Yeah, right," she said in obvious disbelief as she hacked away at the apple, taking off much more than just the peel. "It was your fault."

"I know." Jake put his hand on hers, stilling her movement. "Maybe you better give me the knife before you hurt someone."

"I'm busy. Leave me alone."

"I wish I could," he said huskily.

The knife fell from her grip, and he put a hand on her shoulder and turned her around. "You're driving me crazy," he said, reaching out to touch her cheek. "So soft. So incredibly soft."

She turned her face into his palm in a warm, trusting gesture that seduced him more than anything she could have said or done.

"Maggie," he said, caressing her name with the tip of his tongue.

"What?" she murmured. "What do you want from me?"

Chapter Seven

Jake stared at her, suddenly realizing that what he wanted from her he definitely could not have. He stepped away and walked over to the window, taking several deep breaths as he did so. When his emotions were firmly back under control, he turned to look at her.

She had resumed her apple peeling, but her hands were still unsteady, telling him that she was probably feeling at least a little of what he was feeling. He had to put a stop to things before they both got carried away.

"Aunt Ida told you that I'm here to help her with the hotel, right?" he said.

Maggie paused at the change of subject and then looked at him. "She mentioned something to that effect. But I don't know the details."

"The details aren't important. What is important is helping Aunt Ida get things straightened out."

"I understand that, but why the secrecy?"

"Aunt Ida has a flair for the dramatic."

She looked at him uncertainly. "Is that all it is?"

"I can't tell you any more. It would put you in an even worse position than you're in right now."

"That doesn't seem possible," Maggie said grimly, getting back to her peeling. "Mr. Stone is dying to fire me for the slightest reason. Seeing me with you yesterday was the last straw. He's put me on final warning."

Jake pulled out a kitchen chair and sat on it backward, resting his arms on the back edge. "Why does old Stoneface hate you so much?"

"Heck if I know." She paused. "Sometimes I get distracted at the front desk. I start talking to the guests and get caught up in their lives. I can't help it. People tell me their problems and when I try to help, I get myself in hot water. Like with Mrs. Kensington's dog."

Jake smiled. "That sounds like a good story."

Maggie frowned. "More like a nightmare. Mrs. Kensington had a poodle that she treated like a son. This dog lived better than I do. He was supposed to stay with her sister but then her sister got sick, and she needed to have the dog stay at the hotel with her."

"Which is definitely against the rules," Jake said sternly, but his lips curved into a smile.

Maggie's shoulders straightened in defense. "The poor dog would have been all alone, and Mrs. Kensington was really upset. It was her eighty-fifth birthday, and except for her sister, Strauss—that was the name of her poodle—was her only family."

"What did you do?"

"I snuck the dog into the hotel."

"And you got caught, of course."

"Of course, because bad luck seems to follow me around." Maggie paused in her peeling to face him.

"Everything was perfect. I had the dog stashed under a food-service table, and made it into the elevator with no problems. And then what happens? The elevator gets stuck. Me and Strauss were in there for fifteen minutes. He ate all the food on the table. Then he had an accident on the floor."

Jake burst out laughing and Maggie reluctantly grinned as she shook her finger at him. "It wasn't funny then. When the doors opened, there was Mr. Stone and Mrs. Kensington, who had told everyone in the world that her dog was stuck on the elevator. That's when I got my first warning."

"I wish I could have seen you."

"The point is I was just trying to help."

"At least you made Mrs. Kensington happy," Jake said.

"No. She was furious that Strauss had hamburger for lunch. Said something about his cholesterol count."

"Maybe you should find another job," Jake suggested. "Something less restrictive."

"No way. I need this job. My house, remember. I almost have the down payment. Anyway, what are you hanging around here for?" Maggie demanded. "Can't you see I'm busy?"

"I'm curious. I want to see what you do that makes your pie come out so terrible."

"I prefer to fail in private."

"Maybe I can help." Jake stood up and pushed the chair back against the table.

Maggie looked at him in astonishment. He was wearing his usual blue jeans and cowboy boots. His short-sleeved T-shirt revealed tanned muscular arms. He looked like a man who could wrestle a steer to the ground, not one who would be remotely interested in cooking. "You've made apple pie?" she asked finally, her mouth dropping open in surprise.

"Dozens of times," he said. Grinning, he reached out and gently pressed her jaw back up. "You were catching flies, honey."

"I, uh, I can't believe someone like you can cook."

"I'm a jack-of-all-trades. Where's the recipe?"

Maggie pointed to the three scraps of paper. Without further ado, Jake washed his hands in the sink and started checking through her ingredients.

"I've already got the dough ready," she said, feeling as if she had somehow lost control of the situation.

"Good, then we just have to make the filling."

"I'll get you the measuring spoons."

Jake shook his head. "Don't need those. I prefer to go with my gut instinct."

"You can't cook by gut instinct."

"Of course you can, that's the secret."

Maggie stared at him in disbelief. "My mother always measured. At least I think she did. Although I've never been able to figure out a pinch of this and a dab of that.

"Who did the cooking after your mom died?" Jake asked as he mixed the sugar and apples together.

"We divided it up by the day. My dad was a great one for making charts. Everyone took a turn. But we never had anything fancy, just steak and potatoes, chicken and rice, things like that." Maggie paused, leaning against the counter as she watched his quick, efficient movements. "Did your mother teach you to cook?"

Jake uttered a short, harsh laugh. "My mother couldn't make tea. We had a housekeeper. Gracie Butterworth." He smiled at the mention of her name. "She was a huge woman, loved her own cooking and had the biggest heart of anyone I've ever known. I used to hang out with her after school. I guess I picked up a few things along the way."

Maggie thought about what he had said, reading between the lines of bravado and seeing a shy, insecure boy. Was that really possible? Was the rebellious, charming Jake Hollister a lonely kid at heart? No, her imagination was simply running away with her as usual.

"Were you an only child?" she asked curiously.

"Yes, thank God."

"Why do you say it like that? Weren't you and your parents close?"

"Oh, we were close, all right." His voice turned bitter. "My parents were on my back from the minute I was born until I got my divorce two years ago. They had plans for me, you see. Big plans. I could either go into my mother's family business, the Castleton Hotel Chain, or I could take over my father's Fortune 500 electronics company."

"Wow," Maggie said.

Jake looked over at her and smiled. "Exactly how I felt. I did the routine for a while, got straight A's in school, graduated from Harvard, got an MBA and bought my first rack of Italian suits. I even married the perfect woman—beautiful, smart and ambitious enough for both of us." His lips tightened into a hard line. "God, I made a lot of mistakes. And why the hell am I telling you all this for? Where's the cornstarch?"

Maggie pointed to the box on the far edge of the counter. "So, now you ride a motorcycle, wear blue jeans and don't work except for some covert operations for your aunt."

"That's about it." He poured the filling into the pie shell. "Is the oven preheated?"

"Yes," Maggie said, somewhat bemused as she looked down at the pie. "How did you do that so fast?"

"Cooking has always been my therapy. And believe me, where I come from, therapy is definitely necessary." He set the pie in the oven, adjusted the temperature and wiped his hands on the towel. "Now, we just have to wait. There's nothing like the smell of apple pie baking in the oven."

"I can't imagine you smell it that often if you're always on the road," Maggie said pointedly.

"Once in a while, I hole up somewhere and bake. But don't tell anyone. It'll ruin my image."

"I thought you didn't care what people thought."

"I don't, unless their opinion comes with a fist attached to it."

Maggie folded her arms across her chest. "You're not so tough, are you?"

He grinned. "We both know *you* can take me, although you did have the element of surprise on your side. If you tried it now, there's no way you could get me on my back." He paused. "Although that idea has some merit."

Maggie drew in a breath as an image of them rolling around on the kitchen floor chased through her head. "Do you want some coffee?" she asked, changing the subject. "Or should I make that ice water?"

"Coffee will be fine," Jake replied, settling himself at the kitchen table.

Maggie poured them each a cup and then sat down across from him. "What did you and Gracie Butterworth talk about in the kitchen?"

"I don't remember. It was a long time ago."

"What happened to her?"

"Nothing. She still works for my parents. They live in Laguna Beach, down south. I haven't been home in a while."

"Why not?"

Jake set his cup down. "You do get caught up in people's lives, don't you?"

"Yes, especially when those people are intriguing." Maggie took a sip of coffee and for a moment they just sat there, staring at each other. The only sound in the room was their breathing, in unison and then apart, evoking all kinds of erotic thoughts in her head. God, she was losing it. Getting turned on by simply hearing the man breathe. She had to get out more often.

"I better go," Jake said finally, setting down his cup on the table.

Maggie immediately protested, realizing how much she wanted him to stay. "But you have to taste your pie."

"This isn't a good idea. You and me..."

"What? You and me, what?" She looked at him searchingly, seeing more than just his rough, tough exterior. His brief confidence had let her inside his head, and she had seen loneliness, yearning, feelings that were as familiar to her as her own skin. She wanted this man, and he seemed to want her, but there was so much to risk. So much to lose.

Jake stood up with a jerk, his chair grating along the floor from the thrust of his body. His breathing was loud and ragged, and Maggie felt her own heart beating in accompaniment. He was either going to storm out the door or take her in his arms and kiss her senseless.

Unconsciously, she got to her feet, closing the distance between them, barricading his way out. He put his hands on her shoulders and looked down into her face with an intensity that made her feel as if he were memorizing every feature. Then he thrust her away from him and headed toward the door.

He opened it so hard, the person standing on the other side nearly fell through the doorway. Jake jumped back and Maggie gasped at the intrusion. She had been so caught up in Jake that the rest of the world had ceased to exist. Now it was back.

Antonio Pastorini, sixty-some years young with gray-black hair and the olive skin of his Italian ancestors, put a hand on the doorjamb to steady himself.

"Mr. Pastorini. I didn't hear you knock," Maggie said.

Antonio pointed a bony finger at Jake. "I was just about to when he opened the door."

"What can I do for you?" Maggie asked.

Antonio sighed heavily and waved his hand around in the air. "This city is crazy. I can't take it no more. I'm moving to Miami to live with my sister."

"Miami. That sounds nice," she said faintly, trying to figure out how to handle what was potentially a delicate situation.

"Maggie," Jake interrupted. "I'll head out now—"

"Wait," she said, holding up a hand. She had a feeling she was going to need a friend, and Jake was the closest thing to it at the moment. "I didn't introduce you. This is Antonio Pastorini, my landlord. Jake Hollister."

The two men exchanged nods while Maggie tried desperately to think of some way to calm the volatile Antonio.

"I'm sorry, Maggie, but I have to sell. I can't wait no longer. This heart of mine is going fast."

"Are you sick?" she asked in alarm.

"No, I'm old. Old and tired. I'll just go down to Miami and wait out my last few days," he said dramatically, pulling an old fisherman's hat off his head and holding it against his heart.

Maggie looked at Jake and saw him beat back a smile. For a moment, she felt like smiling, too, until she realized the implication of his words. "But I don't quite have the money together, Mr. Pastorini. I need a few more weeks."

"I got a lady who wants the house, cash in hand. I'd like to sell the house to you, but your payments are late, and my nephew tells me you got into trouble again, no?"

Maggie frowned. Sam Pastorini was a bellboy at the hotel. A bellboy with a big mouth. "It was nothing, a minor misunderstanding. Please, Mr. Pastorini. We have a deal."

"But I worry that if I wait, and you lose your job, I will have no buyer."

Maggie couldn't argue with that concern since it was one she had had many times herself. Antonio had been more than generous, setting up a special payment deal for her, and even when she had been late on payments, he had let it go. But now she was too close to let it slip through her fingers.

"What if I can get all the money sooner?" she asked in desperation. "You'll still give me first crack at buying the house?"

"A week, Maggie. That's all." Antonio gave Jake an assessing look and then walked out the door.

Maggie sank down on the chair, taken aback by this new development. Her mind was racing in a hundred different directions, and she looked up at Jake in desperation. "Where am I going to get eight thousand dollars in a week?'' She stood up and paced restlessly around the room.

"Maybe your father?"

"No. Absolutely not. His money always comes with strings, and that's the last thing I need."

"Okay. How about the bank?"

Maggie rolled her eyes. "This is my third job in the last two years, Jake. And I'm on probation. I doubt the bank would see me as a good risk."

Jake frowned. "I'd like to set things straight with Harry Stone for you, but Aunt Ida made me promise to wait. It's only a few days. Nothing is going to happen to your job at the hotel. You have to believe that."

"I'd like to, but right now I feel like I'm caught between a rock and a hard place."

"Maybe I could lend you the money," Jake said finally, not quite meeting her eyes.

Maggie looked at his averted gaze, his hard profile, and knew she couldn't accept his offer. "No, thanks. We hardly know each other. I couldn't ask you for eight thousand dollars. I don't even know if you have eight thousand dollars."

"I could probably scrape it up if I had to."

"But you don't have to. This is my problem." She shook her head. "I want this house so I can be independent. Getting someone to bail me out isn't going to work."

"You don't need a house to be independent. In fact, you'd probably feel a lot more free if you didn't have it. Tying yourself down to four walls and a roof isn't all it's cracked up to be," he said.

Maggie planted her hands on her hips and glared at him. "What is your problem, Jake? Did you get dumped by a real estate agent? You have the strangest attitude about owning property. Most people would love to own a home."

Jake smiled cynically. "I spent years of my life working for a house, Maggie. It had to be big and perfect and better than anyone else's. It had to be in the right location and then it had to have the trendiest furnishings and the best art." He shook his head. "It was all worth nothing in the end, gone faster than I could have imagined."

"What happened?"

"A fire. Flames consumed the house faster than I could lick an ice cream down to the cone." He snapped his fingers. "*Poof,* it was gone."

"You didn't want to rebuild?"

"There was nothing left to rebuild."

"But there's always—"

"There was nothing. Believe me."

Maggie wanted to ask more questions, to find out how the fire had started and what had happened to his wife, but the set expression on Jake's face along with the lingering pain in his eyes kept her quiet. "I'm sorry."

"Forget it. Tell me more about your landlord, Maggie. Maybe we can figure out another solution."

She shrugged, feeling hopeless at the thought. "What's to tell? He's a widower. He and his wife used to live here, but when she died, he moved out and took an apartment. He threatens to sell every couple of months. When he gets depressed, he wants to move. He's a wonderful man but lonely."

"Ahh," Jake uttered thoughtfully, sitting back in his chair. "Mr. Pastorini is lonely. That's your problem. If you could cheer him up, then maybe he'd decide to stay here long enough for you to get the money together. Yes, that's the ticket."

"I suppose," she said doubtfully, watching the mischievous expression cross his face. "What are you thinking, Jake?"

"I've got the perfect solution to your problem." He laughed out loud. "And to mine. This is great."

"What are you talking about?"

"We'll make Mr. Pastorini happy. We'll find someone that he can talk to. And I know just the person."

Maggie looked at him warningly. "You wouldn't."

"She owes us big-time."

"She'll say no."

"I won't give her the chance." He reached out and grabbed Maggie in his arms, squeezing her with delight. "You and I are going to set up Aunt Ida and Antonio Pastorini. It's a match made in heaven."

"Well . . . it just might work," Maggie said, getting caught up in his excitement. "At least we can keep him busy for a few days. Oh, thank you, Jake. Thank you. Thank you. Thank you. I am so relieved, I could kiss you."

He opened his arms wide. "Go with the feeling, honey. Live for the moment."

Maggie hesitated and then stood on tiptoe so she could kiss him on the mouth. She started out tentative and gained confidence with his immediate response, turning a grateful smooch into something hot and hungry that lasted until the buzzer on the oven went off.

Jake laughed as they broke apart. "I guess we're done."

She grinned at him. "Do you think we're hot enough?"

"Definitely."

"Then it's time for dessert."

"I already had mine," Jake replied, touching her lips with his finger.

"I'm talking about pie."

Maggie walked over to the oven and pulled the pie out. The crust was a golden brown, the insides puffy and smelling like cinnamon, sugar and apples. It was perfect. The day was perfect. He was perfect. A cloud of euphoria encompassed her until she looked over at Jake.

He had opened the refrigerator door and was drinking milk straight out of the carton. No, he wasn't quite perfect. There were some things about him that were downright annoying, but darn if he wasn't the most exciting man she'd come across in a long time.

Jake caught her staring and smiled guiltily. "Sorry."

"Do you want a piece of pie with that?"

"In a minute. We have to figure out how to get Aunt Ida and Mr. Pastorini together."

Maggie pursed her lips together as she thought. "Maybe I could invite them both to dinner."

Jake cleared his throat. "Is your main course better than your pie?"

"Very funny."

"Let's go for pizza instead, something casual."

"Your aunt isn't seeing anyone else, is she?"

"I don't think so, but she doesn't tell me everything."

"Maybe we shouldn't do this. Somebody might get hurt."

"Aunt Ida didn't have any qualms about setting us up," Jake reminded her. "And Mr. Pastorini is about to sell your house out from under you. If you want to have a conscience attack, go right ahead, but it's not going to help."

"All right. We'll do pizza, but it will have to be tomorrow after my day shift."

"Okay. You call up Mr. Pastorini and tell him you want to talk to him about the house over dinner tomorrow. I'll bring along Aunt Ida and we'll meet at the restaurant." His eyes twinkled. "She'll think it's great because you and I are together."

Maggie smiled. He looked like a kid plotting the takeover of a pirate ship. "Sounds good so far. Then what?"

"Then you have a terrible stomachache and want to go home. I'll gallantly offer my assistance and Aunt Ida will be so thrilled to see us leaving together that she won't complain when I suggest she get a ride back from Mr. Pastorini.

Maggie clapped her hands with delight. "Perfect."

"I don't know about perfect, but it's worth a shot." He rubbed his hands together. "Now, I need a taste of that pie before I go." He walked over to the counter and cut a slab of pie, sliding it onto a plate with the back of the knife.

Maggie pulled a fork out of the drawer and handed it to him, watching as he took a bite. "Well?" she demanded.

"Try it." He scooped a chunk of pie onto the edge of his fork and held it out to her.

The intimate gesture brought them very close together, and as Maggie took the piece of pie off the fork, her eyes caught with his. Smiling, laughing eyes that were impossible to resist. Jake Hollister might be irritating, but he was always a good time.

Then her attention switched to the pie, literally melting in her mouth in an array of delicious sensations. "It's wonderful," she said. "Fabulous. What did you do?"

"Chef's secret."

"But how am I going to reproduce it for the fair if you don't tell me?"

"You'll have to be really, really nice to me."

He touched her lip with the edge of his thumb, bringing away a crumb of pie, and Maggie watched in fascination as he licked it off his finger with a promise of what was to come.

Shaking her head, she tried desperately to still the rush of heat that was sweeping through her body. This man was going to drive her crazy if she wasn't careful.

"You don't have to tell me," she said with a hint of panic in her voice. "I'll figure out that recipe without your help. And I can take care of Mr. Pastorini, too."

"What's this? Stubborn pride rearing its ugly head?"

"I don't want you to think that I need your help."

Jake looked at her somberly. "Good. You don't need me. I don't need you. That means we should get along just fine."

"Right." His agreement was what she had wanted, but instead of making her happy, it made her depressed.

"But let me help you with Mr. Pastorini, anyway. It's only a fair return for what you're doing for us at the hotel."

Maggie gratefully conceded the point. "That sounds reasonable."

"You scrub my back, and I'll scrub yours." He lowered his head and whispered in her ear. "And I mean that literally. See you tomorrow night."

Chapter Eight

"Anchovies, onions, mushrooms, the works," Antonio Pastorini declared, looking at the menu in front of him. "I love a good pizza. But nobody makes it like my Angela used to. She had magic fingers." He raised his own fingers to his lips and kissed them for emphasis.

Maggie smiled as she set down her menu. "You must have had a wonderful marriage."

"We fought like two angry alley cats for thirty years. But the passion . . ." His eyes darkened. "Nothing like it." He turned his gaze to her. "Don't settle for less."

"At the moment, getting married is the last thing on my mind."

"Why? You're not getting any younger. In my day, girls were married before they turned twenty. No time to get into bad habits."

"As if the men didn't have any bad habits," she retorted. "I think older is better. You know what you want from yourself and what you want from someone else. You don't get carried away by raging hormones."

"A little raging is good for the soul," he declared. "Keeps the blood thin. Doesn't clot up on you."

"I doubt that a medical doctor would agree with you."

"What do they know? I'm an old man. I've been around the block, you know what I mean." He looked pointedly at her. "And I saw the way that young man was looking at you this morning. The way you were looking at him."

"Jake?" Maggie laughed nervously. "He's just a friend, barely that. And he's leaving town in a few days."

"Then you better stop him from going."

It was a thought that had crossed her mind, as well, but Maggie shook her head, a resolute set to her chin. "No, he has his life, and I have mine. We're not at all compatible."

"Compatible, comschmatible," he said, snapping his fingers together. "Bacon and eggs are compatible, but they'll kill you. Take champagne and strawberries, two different things, together perfection."

Maggie shook her head. "Could we get off food and back to why we're here?"

"You haven't told me why we're here."

"I want to talk to you about the house."

"Oh, so you're going to soften me up with pizza first. You should have tried lasagna if you really wanted to get to me."

"I'll save that for next time." She paused, her face turning serious. "I need a few more weeks, Mr. Pastorini. Can't you postpone moving to Miami for a while longer?"

"There's nothing for me here," he said somewhat heavily. "No family. Most of my friends are dead. I'm almost there myself. Might as well spend my last days on a beach, see some palm trees, some bikinis."

Maggie shook her head as a smile crossed her lips. "If you can still appreciate a good bikini, I think you have some life left in you. Besides, Napa is your home. I'd hate to see you leave."

"At least not until you get your house."

"Not just that," she said softly, feeling genuine compassion for his plight. "I like you."

He cleared his throat with a rough cough. "We better order, before I choke on all this sweet talk."

As Antonio finished speaking, the outer door opened, and Jake walked in with Ida Castleton on his arm. They made quite a pair, Jake in black jeans and a dark purple sweater and Ida in white stretch pants and a glitter-gold top that set off the sparkle in her eyes, the usual glowing smile on her face.

Out of the corner of her eye, Maggie saw Mr. Pastorini stiffen and sit up straighter in his chair, suddenly gaining a few inches of height and confidence. But then he swung his head in her direction and gave Maggie a sharp look. "What are you up to?"

"I don't know what you're talking about." Maggie smiled back with as much innocence as she could muster. "What a coincidence. There's Jake." She waved and Jake nodded, whispering something in his aunt's ear as they made their way across the room.

Antonio stood up as Jake and Ida walked over to the table. Maggie jumped to her feet as well, feeling more than a little nervous now that the setup was at hand.

"Hello, dear," Ida said with a charming smile. "I didn't expect to see you here tonight."

Maggie cleared her throat, prepared to offer some rational excuse, but she didn't have a chance, because Ida had already turned her attention to Antonio.

"I'm Ida Castleton," she said, holding out her hand.

Antonio gently squeezed her hand as he gazed into her eyes. Finally, he spoke in a gruff voice. "Antonio Pastorini. It's a pleasure to finally meet you."

"Finally?" she murmured, a question in her voice.

"My nephew Sam works at your hotel. He says you are a fine woman, and I have seen you sometimes—in the distance."

Ida flushed at the compliment, and Maggie and Jake exchanged an amused look. Then Jake maneuvered his aunt so that she was soon seated next to Antonio.

"Are you a friend of Maggie's?" Ida asked.

"He's my landlord," Maggie interjected.

"Oh. You own the house that Maggie wants so badly." Ida nodded her head in understanding. "She talks about that house all the time. I almost think she likes it better than my hotel."

"They don't compare," Maggie said hastily. "This is a simple cottage, but it really is lovely, and I know Mr. Pastorini had many happy years there, too."

"Yes, but I would have lived anywhere with Angela. My wife," he said to Ida Castleton. "She died five years ago, bless her soul."

"I lost my husband almost a decade ago, but I still have the memories. I thank God for those," Ida said in commiseration.

"Have you two ordered?" Jake interrupted.

"We were just about to," Maggie replied, almost sorry he had broken up the conversation. But they had plenty of time to push Ida and Antonio together, at least for the evening. "Mr. Pastorini likes anchovies," she added.

"So do I," Ida said, clapping her hands in delight. "In fact, I adore them, and I never get to eat pizza with anyone who likes them."

"Ah, a woman who understands food." Antonio shook his head in amazement. "You never married again?"

Ida shook her head. "No, I never found anyone else I could really talk to. It's so difficult, especially at my age."

"I know what you mean," he said nodding in understanding. "Single women of my generation are not too many, at least ones that still want to have some fun. I got plenty of time later to sit in my chair and do crossword puzzles. Now—" he paused "—now, I'd rather go dancing."

"Me, too," she said with a grin.

"Ahem," Jake said, clearing his throat. "I'm going to order the pizza now. Maybe we should go half-and-half on the anchovies. They're not high on my list of favorites."

"Try something new, honey," Ida said. "I hope you don't mind our joining you, Maggie. But since we're all here..."

Maggie shook her head. "No, not at all. I forgot I'd mentioned this place to Jake when he asked about pizza."

"I'm glad you told him about it. I do love a party," Ida replied, turning her bright smile on Antonio.

Maggie watched as the older man lit up under that beacon. As Jake went up to the counter to place their order, Ida and Antonio started talking about the history of the restaurant and their younger days in Napa.

Maggie couldn't believe how well it was all going. Ida was charming and Antonio was responsive. Jake was getting pizza, and she was feeling like a third wheel.

"I was a contractor, could fix anything, build any house in the world," Antonio boasted. "Then I get old and everyone wants a young, strong man." He pointed to his thin arms. "I may not have the muscle, but I've got the brain," he added, moving his finger to his head.

"Experience counts far more than muscle," Ida agreed. "In fact, I have a young man who is supposed to remodel my suite, but he can't seem to understand the way I want to do things. He keeps trying to change my mind."

"Ah, but the customer is always right," Antonio replied.

"My thoughts exactly."

"Pizza will be out in fifteen minutes," Jake announced, returning to the table. "How about a pitcher of beer to go with our meal? Or would you rather have wine?"

"Whatever you want, dear," Ida said, dismissing him with a wave of her hand.

Jake shrugged and walked over to the bar.

"The thing I'm really concerned about is closet space, Antonio," Ida continued. "You don't mind if I call you Antonio, do you?"

"Of course not."

"And please call me Ida. Now, what do you think of those new closet inserts, where you get the shelves and some hooks to make more room out of the closet?"

Antonio shook his head. "Better to customize. Build everything yourself. Then you get it exactly the way you want it."

"Maybe Mr. Pastorini could give you some suggestions," Maggie interjected.

"That's a wonderful idea. If you have the time, of course," Ida added.

Antonio straightened in his chair, confidence filling his body, making him look bigger and more impressive. "It would be a pleasure."

"But don't forget you're planning to move to Miami next week," Maggie said. "You won't have much time."

Antonio tipped his head. "Perhaps I can push it back a day or two for a lady as lovely as this."

Ida laughed. "Oh, you are a charmer. I really would love your help. It's so difficult to find a genuine craftsman these days." She paused, her gaze drifting over to the bar where Jake was standing and then back to Maggie and finally to Antonio. "I wonder—do you think we could do it now?"

"Now?" Maggie asked in surprise, but Ida ignored her and turned to Antonio with a determined smile.

"I'm not really hungry for pizza. And I have a chef at the hotel who makes the most wonderful lasagna you have ever tasted. Garlic bread, too."

Antonio threw up his hands. "Lasagna is my favorite. I would love to come."

Maggie's mouth dropped open as they stood up. "But, but—what about the pizza?"

"You and Jake have it. My nephew will only be around for a few more days," she said to Antonio. "I'm sure these two young people don't need us around."

Jake walked back to the table as Maggie got to her feet. "What's going on?" he asked.

"Mr. Pastorini is going to drive me back to the hotel and take a look at remodeling my suite," Ida said. You can give Maggie a ride home."

Jake looked as stunned as Maggie felt. "I thought we were having dinner together. You wanted to talk about the hotel, remember?"

"Oh, we can do that tomorrow. You don't mind, do you?" Without waiting for an answer, Ida slipped her hand through Mr. Pastorini's arm and they walked out of the restaurant.

"We've been stood up," Maggie said in amazement. "I can't believe it."

Jake shook his head. "She did it again. Fixed it so we would have to be alone together." He tried to look angry, but his smile got in the way and eventually a laugh broke from his lips. "She is a devil."

"At least they're together. Part of our plan worked." Maggie sat back down in her chair and sipped the beer that Jake had brought for her. "What do you want to do now?"

"Considering that I just forked over thirty bucks for pizza, I guess we better wait for it. Looks like we're stuck with each other for a while."

"Guess so." Maggie took another sip of beer. "I couldn't believe how fast they hit it off. I didn't say a word, just sat here and watched them flirt with each other like two love-struck kids."

Jake smiled. "Aunt Ida has always enjoyed men."

"And Mr. Pastorini moves a lot faster than I thought."

"Hopefully, he'll stay interested long enough to delay his move to Miami, and you'll be able to get your house."

The house. Maggie had almost forgotten her original goal. "It would be nice if they got together, even aside from the house," she said. "I mean, they're both single and a little lonely. They might be good for each other."

"Not you, too," he groaned, rolling his eyes. "Why do women always want to set other people up?"

"Hey, this was your idea," she reminded him. "I just went along with it."

"I know. And Aunt Ida outsmarted both of us."

Maggie stiffened. "We don't have to stay, you know. We can just get the pizza and go home. In fact, I can get a cab right now." She started to get to her feet, but he pulled her back down.

"Whoa, honey. Put the brakes on. First tell me what I said or didn't say to get you in such a mood."

"I'm not in a mood, but it's obvious that you're not interested in my company. You're practically fuming because Mrs. Castleton left us here alone. I know when I'm not wanted."

"No, you don't. You don't know anything." He looked around and then lowered his voice. "I want your company and your conversation and your body and anything else you might like to share. But I don't want you to feel pushed into it courtesy of my aunt."

Maggie stared at him, her mind still stuck on his reference to her body. "I don't," she said finally. "Feel pushed, I mean. We ought to be able to share a pizza without any major problems."

"I'm not worried about the pizza. I'm more concerned about driving you home and saying good-night at the door when what I really want to do is stay—all night."

Maggie didn't know what to say to such a candid statement or how to respond to such an intense look. Jake certainly didn't wrap his desires up in pretty sentences.

She looked down at her beer and took another drink for courage. "I don't know what to say, Jake."

He sat back in his chair. "Say no. Say I hate your guts and I don't want anything to do with you."

"Why?"

"Because it's safer that way, and you, Maggie, are the kind of woman who should definitely play it safe."

Her temper flared at his comment. "You don't know what kind of woman I am. I'm tougher than I look."

"Not on the inside, Maggie. You're one of the gentlest individuals I know, kind, caring, concerned about people. And I wouldn't want to hurt that."

"What makes you think you could? I'd have to care about someone to be hurt by them," she said defiantly.

Jake ran a hand through his hair and sighed. "Look, let's talk about something else. In fact, let's not talk. I challenge you to a game of pool."

Maggie followed his gaze to the back room where a pool table was surrounded by video arcade games. "I don't know how to play pool."

"I'll teach you."

She looked at him curiously. "Where did you learn to play pool? From Gracie Butterworth?"

"No, from Rico, the chauffeur." Jake sent her a mischievous grin. "He was supposed to take me to the library when Mother was at the beauty salon. But instead, we'd go to the pool hall. I learned a hell of a lot more there than I could have learned at the library." He stood up. "What do you say?"

Maggie hesitated. The last thing she wanted was to get into another situation where Jake was the master and she was the novice. She was getting a little tired of coming in second. Her gaze drifted around the room and settled on the dart board. "I have a better idea," she said. "Darts."

"Darts?" Jake echoed.

"Yes." Throwing a steel-pointed tip at a target seemed like a very good idea. Maybe she could get rid of some of her frustration. She pushed back the chair and got up.

"Okay. You're on," Jake said as he followed her over to the dart board.

Maggie pulled the darts out of the board. "I'll let you go first," she said. "Loser buys dinner."

"Oh, we're going to put some money on this, are we?"

"Are you game?"

"Sure, why not?" Jake lined up, pulled his hand back, took careful aim and let go. The dart missed the bull's-eye by a good inch. His next throw was a little bit closer and his final throw was sidetracked by Maggie's discreet cough. He threw her a dirty look. "You did that on purpose!"

"I wouldn't. Not me, I'm kind and caring, remember?"

"I should have mentioned proud and competitive in that description."

Maggie smiled sweetly and moved his darts out of the way. "My turn." Taking a step back, she fired the first dot with the precision of a master rifleman. Bull's-eye. Her next shot followed the same rocket path, as the two points of the darts were married together. Her third shot followed the pattern, a triple bull's-eye.

Jake looked at her in stunned amazement. "You just hustled me."

"Would I do that? Sweet little me?"

"What do you do—practice darts every night before you go to bed?"

"Yes, and sometimes I use people's pictures for target practice."

"Ouch," Jake said with a smile. "But I don't think you have my picture, do you?"

"If I don't have a picture, I just imagine where the steel tip of the dart is going to strike on their body." Maggie burst out laughing as Jake took a surreptitious look at his lower body.

"Okay, I left out mean and nasty in my earlier description," Jake said, taking her by the hand. "No more darts for you. We better play something safer."

"But you're not a man who likes to play it safe," she said daringly. "Remember?"

"No, but I do like to keep all my body parts intact."

When they reached the table, Maggie sat down, picked up her beer and drained it to the last drop. She was feeling better after her victory, more in control of the situation.

"Do you want another glass of beer?" Jake asked.

"No, thanks. I think I'll wait for the pizza."

"I suppose your brothers taught you how to play darts."

"Yes. And it was one of the few things I could do better than them. I thrived on it."

He looked at her curiously. "I'm surprised your dad didn't get you into the service in some capacity."

"He didn't want to, in the beginning. He never had much use for women in the service. Thought they should be at home having babies. But he's mellowed a lot in the last few years. He called me the other day and told me my brother Mike is getting married to a woman in the service. He sounded thrilled." She shook her head. "Sometimes I can't figure him out. He seems to want one thing but then he changes his mind about it. I'll never be able to please him, no matter what I do."

"Is pleasing him that important to you?"

Maggie shrugged, trying to look more casual than she felt. "Everyone wants to please their dad. Didn't you?"

"Another impossibility," Jake admitted with a twist of his lips. "Like your father, my old man was tough. Nothing was good enough."

"I used to blame my dad for the way we had to live," Maggie continued, fiddling with her empty glass. "I was a shy kid, and it was difficult to make new friends everywhere."

"Which is why you now want to spend the rest of your life in one place, behind a picket fence, baking pies and growing zucchini."

Maggie looked up at him. "I know that sounds silly. But it's all I've ever wanted, to have a home, to be the same place in the summer that I was in the winter."

Jake took a sip of his beer and set his glass down. "Any husbands in the picture?"

"Not right now, but someday the right man will come along."

"He'll have to, because you won't be going anywhere."

"There's nothing wrong with wanting some permanency in your life. I've done it the other way and it's not all it's cracked up to be."

"That was different. You were a kid. You had no control. But now you're an adult. You can live wherever you want to live. Why restrict yourself to one house, one town? I like being able to go where the mood takes me, be my own man. You should try it.''

Maggie rested her elbows on the table and studied him. ''But is this biker guy really you, Jake? I get the feeling you hide a lot under that tough exterior.''

Jake leaned forward until their heads were only a few inches apart. ''I get that same feeling about you, Maggie. Maybe we're both trying to hide.''

''I'm not,'' she whispered.

''You're a dreamer, Maggie, and deep down you like adventure. I can't believe you're going to satisfy those needs by spending your whole life in a small town.''

''And are you going to be satisfied spending your life on the road, doing odd jobs when you have a brilliant mind and an MBA from Harvard to go with it?'' she challenged.

Emotion sizzled between them as Jake looked into her eyes, into her mind, into her heart. She didn't know what he saw in her face, but she saw nothing in his. A mask had fallen over his eyes, even his facial muscles had turned to stone.

Finally, Jake spoke in a quiet but tense tone. ''I'm happy, Maggie, just the way I am.''

''So am I,'' she said defiantly, tilting her chin up like a warrior going to battle.

''Good. At least we agree on one thing.'' He sat back in his chair and folded his arms across his chest.

Maggie did the same. ''Right, we agree.''

At that moment, a teenager brought their pizza over to the table. He slid the pizza onto the middle of the table and set down two plates.

Maggie stared down at the pizza and then into Jake's stunned face. Their eyes connected with the same thought even as their voices chorused. ''Anchovies.''

Jake burst out laughing. "Looks like there's one more thing we agree on," he said, pushing the pizza aside. "I can't eat that."

"Neither can I."

Jake looked at her and Maggie looked back. "Are you thinking what I'm thinking?" she asked.

"Ice cream."

"Ice cream," she echoed, nodding her head.

He raised an eyebrow and lowered his voice. "Let's make it an afternoon delight, Maggie. Come on, let's do it."

Her heart caught, not at his words, but at the implication. "It's evening," she murmured.

Jake stood up and held out his hand. "Use your imagination."

Chapter Nine

Maggie settled for a single scoop of vanilla and another sleepless night where her imagination ran wild.

Imagining Jake in her house, in her life, in her bed wasn't difficult at all. Getting him out of her imagination was a lot tougher, she decided the next day, as she finished checking in a guest at the hotel. Of course, it didn't help to see him every time she turned around. Since she'd come on duty at three o'clock, he'd come by the desk to check for messages, sat in the lobby reading a newspaper and finally jogged by in a pair of indecent navy blue running shorts and tank T-shirt as he headed for the outdoor track that wound along the hotel.

Her blood pressure had gone up with each appearance and was now threatening to blow sky-high. But she had to keep a lid on it. Jake might be watching her, but so was Mr. Stone, and at the moment her manager had to be her first consideration.

As if on cue, the door behind her opened and she looked up as Harry Stone walked out with Karen Monte.

"Miss Gordon, there's going to be someone from the home office coming out to check on our operations," Harry said.

Maggie nodded casually, trying to correlate this information with what she already knew.

"I hope I don't have to remind you to be on your best behavior. There are to be no slipups."

"Of course," she murmured. "Do you know who's coming?"

"That's not important. We treat all our guests equally," he replied smoothly. "However—" he looked around as he lowered his voice. "—if you could persuade your *friend* to leave a few days early, that would be appreciated."

Maggie stared him in dismay. "I don't have any control over Mr. Hollister's movements. We barely know each other."

"Another thing," Harry said, ignoring her response, "the senior staff is going to have a dinner meeting tonight with Mrs. Castleton. You'll have to hold down the front desk on your own for about an hour."

"That's fine." Maggie let out a sigh of relief when Harry returned to his office. She turned to Karen. "I won't mind having him out of my shadow for a few hours."

"I know what you mean. Mr. Stone has always been strict, but in the last few weeks, he's gotten almost crazy about routine, and he certainly doesn't like you."

"He's made that perfectly clear. I just don't know why. I've made a few mistakes, but nothing that terrible."

Karen shrugged. "I wish I could help, but lately he's like a volcano ready to erupt. Maybe things will settle down once this surprise inspection is over."

"Maybe," Maggie said faintly, wondering what Karen would say if she knew Jake was the undercover guest. Fortunately, a guest stepped up to the desk and she was able to get her mind off Jake and back on to work. The next hour passed uneventfully as she went about her daily routine of checking guests in and out of the hotel, taking messages and directing people to the appropriate services. It was after five when Karen interrupted her with a cup of coffee.

"Break time," Karen said, setting a cup down on the counter.

"Thanks," Maggie took a sip and slipped one foot out of her high-heeled pump for a momentary breather.

"How's the pie coming? Doesn't the fair open tomorrow?"

"Yes, and the pie is not quite there yet. I may have to forego the apple pie contest, and settle on entering Henry in the zucchini competition. There's always next year. I won't be going anywhere." Maggie looked over at the manager's office with a frown. "At least I hope not."

Karen grinned. "I hope not, either. You bring a lot of life into this place."

"Not intentionally."

"You know, Maggie, being the perfect homemaker may not be your fate. Not everyone is cut out to stay home and sew curtains." She raised a hand as Maggie started to interrupt. "I'm not saying there's anything wrong with it. My sister does it every day and loves it, but she's married with kids and very satisfied to stay home and build her nest."

"That's just what I want to do, build a cozy nest."

"And then what? For goodness sakes, you're single. You're attractive. You should want more from life."

Maggie sighed. It didn't help to hear Karen state her own doubts so bluntly. Lately, she was beginning to want more from life. But that was because of Jake. He had stormed into her life like a whirlwind, but when he was gone, the dust would settle, and she'd be left with what was important. Her home. Her life. Her heart. Or at least what was left of her heart.

"So, tell me," Karen continued, as she unwrapped a candy bar from one of the drawers. "What's going on with you and James Dean?"

"Nothing."

"That's not what I hear."

"I see the hotel grapevine is in good working order."

"We're like family around here, Maggie. Just pretend I'm your sister and fess up."

Maggie smiled. "If we were family, Mr. Stone would have to be the evil uncle. He practically fired me for taking Jake around to the local wineries. It was an innocent outing. No big deal."

Karen looked at her doubtfully. "If you say so."

Maggie threw up her hands in frustration. "Why doesn't anyone believe me?"

"Because Jake Hollister is anything but innocent."

"I admit he's an interesting guy, but he's not my type."

"He's not cut out to share your gingerbread house."

"Exactly."

"Even so, if I were you, I wouldn't mind hitching on the back of his motorcycle for a short ride."

"That's all it would be, a short ride," Maggie said abruptly. "I want someone who will stick around for the long term. Someone solid and stable and—"

"Boring," Karen finished. "At least this guy would be exciting. He'd be someone to remember the rest of your life."

"He'd *ruin* the rest of my life." Maggie punched a code into the computer and read the file on Jake Hollister. "Look at this. He's leaving next Tuesday. Even if I wanted something to happen, there isn't time."

"You have five more days."

"That's hardly enough time in which to develop a relationship. No, as far as I'm concerned, he can't leave a minute too soon."

She looked up as the front door opened and Jake jogged in, a terry-cloth towel swung around his neck, his muscles gleaming with a fine sheen of sweat.

"Hi, ladies," he said.

Maggie swallowed hard, and Karen burst out laughing as soon as Jake jogged onto the elevator.

"You have it bad, Maggie. Real bad."

Jake leaned against the side of the elevator and watched as the numbers lit up with each floor. When the doors opened, he stepped out and walked slowly down the hall, his jaunty jog completely gone now that he was alone. As he leaned over to insert the key card into the lock, he groaned at his aching muscles. He wasn't an athlete. Who was he kidding? Two miles around the track, and he felt as if he were going to have a coronary. So much for his macho image.

He walked into his room, flung the towel onto a chair and flopped down on his bed. He'd be hurting tomorrow even worse than today and all because of a stupid desire to impress Maggie Gordon. He felt like a nerdy kid trying to get the prom queen's attention. It hadn't worked in high school, and it certainly hadn't worked now.

His body had changed along with his image and his attitude, but deep down, he still didn't feel that he measured up. Probably due to years of seeing the disappointment in his parents' eyes when he brought home an A-minus instead of an A. But that was over now. He was done with trying to impress people, trying to be someone that he wasn't.

As he stared up at the ceiling, the tiles slowly blurred in his mind until all he could see was Maggie's face, her beautiful skin, her warm blue eyes. Images played across his mind: a proud Maggie holding her cherished zucchini in her hand; an angry Maggie, flipping him on his back; a sensuous Maggie, looking into his eyes, kissing him back with a passion hotter than the engine on his bike.

God, she was a vision, an impossible dream. She didn't deserve someone jaded and cynical. She was too innocent, too hopeful, too fresh. He had to get the hell out of the hotel, and fast, before he did something stupid like fall in love.

If only he hadn't made a commitment to Aunt Ida, he'd be on the back of his bike and roaring down the highway faster than Maggie could say zucchini. But instead, he was stuck in an impossible situation. In the past, posing as an undercover guest had been fun, especially since he'd found the leather jacket and motorcycle. He'd snooped around for a few days, made a report and then moved on. But this time, it wasn't that simple. He had made mistake number one in business—getting personally involved with a colleague.

Rolling over, he reached for the files his aunt had given him. As a matter of course, all personnel files were reviewed by Ida Castleton every month. She enjoyed knowing her employees and keeping abreast of their progress.

Maggie's file was lying on top, and although he felt a niggling of guilt, he couldn't help but open it. Skimming past the details of address and social security number, he went straight down to the evaluations. Her first evaluation was fairly good, although there were some concerns about her ability to stay focused on her job.

Running his finger down the sheet, he flipped the page, looking for additional information. The next evaluation was much harsher, having taken place after the poodle incident. But the language used seemed out of proportion to the problem. And that's where the personal attacks began. Citations of her manners, her dress, her attention to the guests, even her day with him.

At the end of the report, Jake was more confused than before, but he was clear on one very important point: Harry Stone did not like Maggie Gordon. In fact, he hated her, and was doing everything possible to get rid of her; Jake just couldn't figure out why. But he was determined to find out.

He slid across the bed, groaning at the pain cutting through his hamstring muscles, but persevering until he reached the phone. Picking it up, he dialed his aunt and waited for her to answer.

"Aunt Ida, it's me. What's the schedule for tonight?"

"I'm taking the senior staff out to dinner at seven o'clock," she replied. "I'll give you the keys before I go."

"Fine. I went through the personnel files you gave me. None of them seems out of the ordinary except for one. Maggie's. What does your manager have against her?"

Ida paused. "Harry has implied that Maggie is flighty and irresponsible, but I can't say that I agree with him."

"Aside from the incident with the dog in the elevator, what exactly has she done wrong?"

"You have the file, Jake. Read it for yourself."

"That's the problem. I am reading it, and it doesn't make sense. There are only mentions of things like dawdling at the front desk, talking too long to a guest, changing someone's room when they complained. None of those things warrant a report. In fact, I think she should be commended for taking such an interest in the guests' welfare."

"You do like her, don't you? I knew it."

Jake groaned. "This isn't about liking Maggie. This is about a very strange personnel report. And there are other things. I spoke to the maid today, asked her where the complimentary soaps and shampoos were. She said they were no longer passing them out or stocking them in the rooms."

"But that doesn't make sense. I know I've seen a purchase order for those supplies."

"Exactly. I want to take a more in-depth look at the books tonight. After you get back, we can sit down and go over the items one by one and make sure that the hotel is really getting everything it's paying for."

"What?" Ida muffled her voice and then came back on the phone. "I'll have to talk to you later, Jake. I'm in the middle of something."

"The middle of what?" Jake asked, hearing another voice in the background. "Is someone there with you?"

"I hardly think that's any of your business."

Jake's suspicion doubled. "It's not Mr. Pastorini, is it?"

"He's a charming man, Jake. I'm so glad you introduced the two of us."

"I didn't do anything. You were the one who whisked him away, another attempt to set me and Maggie up."

"Don't be ridiculous. I didn't know he was going to be there."

"But you took advantage of the situation."

"Not for you, for myself. Antonio has some wonderful ideas for my suite."

"Not just for your suite, I bet. You should be careful, Aunt Ida. He could be a fortune hunter."

"Oh, hush, Jake. I'm too old to worry about that." She lowered her voice. "It's so nice to have someone that I can really talk to, someone who seems to understand me almost better than I understand myself. I get lonely, Jake. Can you understand that?"

Better than she knew. "Just be careful, Aunt Ida. Sometimes you trust people too easily."

"It's the only way I know how to be, honey. And frankly, I'm tired of being careful. I'm going to live for the moment, just like you. Goodbye."

"Bye," Jake grumbled as he hung up the phone. Live for the moment hardly seemed to be his motto these days. If he was living for the moment, he wouldn't be lying on his bed alone, daydreaming about a slightly crazy brunette with the best pair of legs in town. He'd be doing something about it.

But what could he do? He certainly had no intention of ever marrying again, and somehow he didn't think Maggie would settle for anything short-term. He just had to hang on.

A few more days, and he could pack up his duffel bag and hit the road for the next city, the next adventure. But even though he tried to drum up some enthusiasm, he failed miserably. His tired body was declaring mutiny on his brain. He didn't want to keep moving. Life on the road was beginning to lose its luster.

Closing his eyes, he decided to take a nap. That would help clear the cobwebs out of his brain, get him reenergized and back on track. But the last thing he saw before he fell asleep was Maggie's cozy house and her deliciously rumpled king-size bed.

"I'm back," Jake said a few hours later as he paused at the front desk.

Maggie looked up with a frown, but he had a feeling she had known he was there the minute he'd stepped off the elevator. She looked tense and stiff as if she were preparing herself for battle. At least one of them was trying to fight the attraction.

"You know, you look just like someone I know," he continued. "Kathy. But there's only one way for me to tell for sure." He leaned forward and Maggie hastily stepped back.

"Don't you dare," she said, looking wildly around to be sure no one saw him. "You've gotten me into enough trouble already."

"Relax. Old Stoneface is having dinner with my aunt."

"I still don't want any trouble."

"Neither do I."

"Then go away."

Jake tipped his head. "Sorry, but I'm on a mission. I need to check out the manager's office while everyone is gone."

Maggie looked at him in alarm. "I can't let you do that. Mr. Stone locks it up when he leaves, and I don't have access to the keys."

Jake pulled out Ida's keys and swung them in front of her eyes. "Orders from the boss."

Maggie hesitated. "Are you sure about this, Jake? Can't you just wait until Mr. Stone gets back and tell him who you are. He already knows someone is coming down from the home office."

Jake sent her a sharp look. "How does he know that?"

"I have no idea. But he told me he'd appreciate it if I could get rid of you before this person arrived."

Jake grinned at her. "That would be a nice trick."

"It's not funny. It would be so much easier if you would just come clean."

"I'm sorry to put you on the spot. But if Stone knows who I am, he might cover his tracks."

"What tracks? What's going on, Jake?"

"I can't tell you, honey. Now, are you going to let me in this way or should I go through the back door?"

Maggie looked around at the quiet lobby and then lifted the counter partition so Jake could walk inside.

"Be quick, okay. Karen is on a dinner break, but she doesn't usually take too long."

Jake nodded, slipped his key into the manager's office door and walked inside. Maggie stayed by the front counter for a few minutes until her curiosity got the better of her. Since the lobby was still empty, she peeked into the office to find Jake shuffling through Harry's desk.

"What are you doing?" she whispered.

"Looking for something."

"What?"

"Clues."

Maggie glared at him in frustration, but Jake ignored her as his gaze came to rest on a letter. He sat back and read it and then looked up at Maggie. "Stone's wife is divorcing him."

"Jake, you shouldn't be looking at that stuff. It's personal...she is?" Maggie added, curiosity getting the better of her. "He never said a word."

"This might explain a lot," Jake muttered as he jotted down some notes on a piece of paper. Then he flipped through another drawer and pounced on a pile of bank receipts, making additional notations on his report. "That should do it," he said, getting to his feet.

"What did you find out?"

"I don't know yet."

Maggie jumped as the bell on the front desk rang. "Oh, no," she groaned.

"Relax. It's probably just someone who wants to check in. You take care of them, and I'll close up in here. And don't look so guilty. We're not breaking the law. Everything in this office belongs to the Castleton Hotel Chain."

Maggie nodded and backed out of the door, forcing a smile on her face before she turned around. As Jake said, it was simply a woman wanting to check in. Nothing strange about that. When she finished the check-in procedure, Maggie rang for the bellboy to take the woman to her room.

Alone again, she looked up as Jake walked out of the office and locked the door behind him.

"Are you done?" she asked.

"For the moment."

"Then maybe you should leave. I don't think it's a good idea for you to hang around here."

"What time do you get off?"

"Eleven."

"Perfect. I'll meet you then."

She grabbed on his sleeve as he turned to leave. "I'm not meeting you."

"But I need your help."

Maggie shook her head, ignoring the almost irresistible plea in his eyes. "Oh, no. I've done my duty. You're on your own."

"I helped you with Mr. Pastorini, and don't forget the pie."

"Your aunt helped me with Mr. Pastorini, and as for the pie, I still can't bake it right because you won't tell me what you did."

He smiled. "My secret, honey."

"Fine, keep your secret. I'll do it on my own."

"Okay, but I still need your help. Come on, I'll make it worth your while."

"You don't have enough money to make it worth my while."

"I wasn't talking about money."

"Go away, Jake," she said, trying to ignore the tingle of excitement that ran goose bumps down her arm.

"I can't." Grabbing her hand, he yanked her behind a wall, holding her just out of sight of the lobby.

"What do you think you're doing?" she asked breathlessly. "I have to work."

"This will just take a second." He lowered his head and kissed her, his mouth so warm and enticing that she couldn't help but respond. Wrapping his arms around her body, he pulled her up against the hard length of his body, his mouth devouring hers with a hunger that matched her own.

Unconsciously, she slid her arms around his neck, running her fingers through his hair, soaking in the wonderful sensation of being in his arms again. It felt so good, so damn good. She didn't want to let the feeling go, and a sense of desperation swept over her. Time was running out. A few days and he would be gone.

Jake groaned deep down in his throat, a raw, husky sound that set her senses on fire. He broke away from her mouth to trail kisses down the side of her neck, stopping only when her tight collar prohibited any further exploration. When Jake lifted his head, he looked as frustrated as she felt.

"Meet me tonight," he said.

It was tempting. So tempting.

"Say yes."

His tone was more of an order than a request, and years of hearing orders put her back up. She hated being pressured, especially by a man. She was supposed to be calling her own shots. Unfortunately, what she wanted was a little too close to what he wanted for her to get really angry.

"Just tonight?" she asked finally.

Jake paused for a long moment. "I can't answer that question."

"Then I can't meet you tonight."

Jake shook his head, frustration warring with understanding. Finally, he smiled. "What about tomorrow?"

Chapter Ten

What about tomorrow? Tomorrow? Tomorrow? The refrain ran around and around in her mind as Maggie pulled weeds out of her garden the next day. If she'd said yes, she'd be rolling around in a bed with the sexiest man she'd ever met, instead of digging worms out of the ground and trying to make flowers grow in weed-infested earth.

But she'd said no. She always said no. She was boring and straitlaced and as rigid as her marine colonel father. As much as she wanted spontaneity, she was afraid of it, terrified of losing herself in someone else's dream, again.

The roar of an engine down the street startled her, and she sat back on her heels, anticipation warring with worry. What if he asked her again? What if he didn't ask her and simply swept her off her feet and headed for the bedroom?

Her heart started to pound and she put her hand to her chest to still the wayward beat. No, those things only happened in the movies. And Jake was far from the ideal hero, at least for her.

A metallic silver car came into view and her momentary excitement dimmed, replaced by a greater worry as Mr. Pastorini pulled into her driveway and got out.

Reluctantly, Maggie got to her feet, prepared to face the worst. If he was still intent on moving to Miami before she had the money for the down payment, she was in big trouble. She certainly had no legal grounds to stop him from selling to someone else.

Antonio waved when he saw her in the garden and walked over to her. Maggie pulled the dirty gloves off her hands and brushed a strand of sweaty hair from her forehead.

"Hello," she said tentatively, trying to judge his mood by the expression on his face.

He smiled and it spread across his face like wildfire, putting a twinkle in his eyes. He didn't look like a weary old man anymore but someone young and alive and energized.

"Oh, Maggie, I am so happy," he said, putting his hand to his heart. "Such joy I haven't known in years."

"Really?" she asked warily. "Because you're moving?"

"Moving?" He looked at her in confusion and then waved his hand. "No. I've found the perfect woman."

"You have?"

"And I have you to thank for it."

"You do?"

He nodded. "Ida has set my soul on fire."

Maggie smiled at his dramatic words. "I guess the two of you really hit it off then."

"She is one fine woman."

"Yes, she is. I'm very happy for you."

"And for yourself, no?" He laughed and shook a finger at her. "I'm not so old I can't see a setup."

"I just wanted you to see that staying in Napa had possibilities that you might not have considered," Maggie explained.

"Oh the possibilities..." His eyes blazed with new light.

Maggie cleared her throat. "Does this mean I still have a few weeks to complete my payments?"

"Take as long as you need. I'm not going anywhere."

She let out a sigh of relief. "You don't know how happy I am to hear you say that."

"It doesn't matter where I live as long as I have someone to share my life with," he said more somberly. "Time passes so quickly. You can't waste a single second. Now, I have to get back to work. We're going to meet with the architect and draw up the plans for Ida's suite today."

"Good luck," Maggie said as he walked away. At least one problem was solved. She waited for a surge of relief to sweep through her, but it was more a like a drizzle than a surge. Annoyed at her own reaction, she bent back down and reattacked the weeds.

Everything was working out perfectly. If she could hang on to her job long enough to make the last few payments, she'd finally have her house, her dream. Of course, she would still be alone. But that didn't matter, she told herself fiercely. It didn't matter at all.

Jake slid into a chair at the counter and frowned at the man about to serve him. "Hit me, Pete."

"A double or a triple?"

"Triple. Chocolate fudge."

Pete nodded and pulled out the ice-cream scooper. "You're late today."

"I've been busy."

"Yeah? Doing what?" Pete handed him the ice-cream cone and took his money in return.

"It's personal."

"Oh. How *is* Maggie?"

Jake glared at him. "Not that personal."

"Too bad." Pete handed him his change and went to help another customer.

Jake licked his way around the cone, hoping the ice cream would make him feel better. But he was smart enough to know that the pleasure would probably melt as fast as the ice cream. Stuffing himself wasn't going to take away the real hunger pain, the hunger for Maggie.

With one scoop down, he started on the second, listening idly to Pete and another man talking about business on their street. When he heard the Castleton Hotel mentioned, his ears perked up and he swung his head around.

"Had dinner there last night. Toughest piece of meat I ever tasted," the man said.

"Are you talking about the Castleton?" Jake interrupted.

The other man looked at him in surprise. "Yeah, why?"

"I'm staying there. Just wondered if the food is always that bad?"

"Didn't used to be," the man replied, taking his pint of ice cream from Pete's outstretched hand. "Place is going downhill and and the prices are going uphill. Talk to you later, Pete."

Jake popped the last of his cone into his mouth and chewed while he thought about the latest piece of information he had heard. The Castletons had always prided themselves on fine dining in their restaurants. But the breakfast he'd had earlier had been pretty bad, too.

He looked over at Pete with a curious frown. "I bet people tell you a lot, don't they?"

Pete raised an eyebrow. "I'm sort of like the local bartender if that's what you mean."

"What do you know about the Castleton?"

"What's your interest?" Pete returned.

Jake hesitated and then decided he needed another ally in town besides Maggie. "I'm Mrs. Castleton's nephew."

Pete's eyes widened in surprise. "No kidding."

"Truth is, I'm trying to help her figure out why business is down. Any ideas, bartender?"

Pete leaned back against the counter and thought for a moment. "Last week there was a convention in town and a big group came in one afternoon. They were complaining that their rooms wouldn't be ready for hours. Apparently, they couldn't get any satisfaction from the management. You already heard about the food. My business has gone up lately, a lot more people stopping for ice cream."

"Thanks. I think I'm beginning to see the light." Jake paused. "By the way, no one from the hotel knows about my connection with the Castletons. I'm trying to get some honest information."

"No problem. I'm just the ice-cream man. One other thing, Jake. The only person I never see in here is the manager. There must be something wrong with him if he doesn't like ice cream.''

Jake got up from his chair and smiled. "I think you got that right. See ya, bud.''

As Jake walked out of the ice-cream parlor, he paused. He could go back to the hotel and continue his investigation. Or he could go by Maggie's house. She wasn't due in at the hotel until four. Plenty of time to...

No, he wasn't going to think about that. He'd just talk to her, see if he could get any more information on the hotel. It was a business decision. Nothing more. He walked down the street and rounded the corner of a building, bumping right into someone coming from the opposite direction.

By instinct, he threw out his hands to steady the woman, and then the touch set off warning bells in his mind.

Maggie glared at him. "Not you again.''

"You do attract trouble, don't you?''

"Let go of me.''

Jake tried to step back but found his wrist was caught on her sweater. "I'd like to, but...''

Maggie followed his gaze to where the threads of her sweater were tangled around the knob of his watch. "Oh, darn. This is my good sweater.''

Jake moved his free hand to work on the tangle, but when his fingers came into contact with the soft curve of her breast, his mind stopped functioning.

"Did you get it?'' Maggie asked.

He shook his head, his throat too tight to speak. Damn, she was lovely. As beautiful and hot as the sunny day that surrounded them. He didn't want to free his hand. He wanted to wrap the other one around her and lose himself in her arms, in her body.

"Hurry up," she commanded with a hint of desperation in her voice. "People are starting to look."

Jake stared into her big blue eyes and caught his breath at what he saw, the same desire, the same smoke, the same intensity. She might be fighting the attraction, but it was there. He jerked as a woman bumped into him with the side of her bulky purse.

"Jake, please," Maggie said. "This isn't the time or the place."

"I know, but—I'm stuck on you."

She tried not to smile, but her lips curved up in rebellion. "That's not funny."

"Yes, it is, and you better laugh, because right now we need a little humor. Know what I mean?"

"Let me do it." Maggie pushed his hand aside and tried to see the problem. With some deft maneuvering, she finally freed his wrist from her shoulder. "There. You're free."

"Yeah, I'm free." As Jake said the word, a heaviness settled around his heart. "Where are you headed?"

"The fairgrounds. The judging should be over by now."

"You baked the pie yourself?"

"No, but I entered Henry." She started to walk away, but Jake fell into step with her.

"Why don't I come with you?"

Maggie hesitated. "I don't think that's a good idea."

"You're probably right, but let me come, anyway."

Another tempting offer. Was she going to say no to everything this man asked? That would be the wisest move, but at the moment her heart was overriding her brain.

"All right."

Jake looked at her consideringly. "You're awfully agreeable all of a sudden. What's the catch?"

"I don't feel like fighting right now." She shrugged, meeting his direct gaze with one of her own.

"Neither do I. Let's go."

Jake had parked his bike at the edge of the hotel parking lot, and Maggie was able to slip on behind him without arousing any additional attention.

Sliding her legs up against his, she was caught again by an overwhelming rush of desire. Grateful that he was in front of her and couldn't see her face, she closed her eyes and just let the emotions sink in, trying to store every sensation in her mind for the memories she would desperately need in the weeks to come.

"Okay?" he muttered, touching her hands wrapped so tightly around his waist.

"Yes."

Jake started the engine and they headed down the highway. The air brushed past her face in a joyous caress. The sun beat down on her shoulders, warming her to the very core of her soul. The scent of grapes from a local vineyard sent a lush, heady feeling through her head. Everything was so right. So perfect.

As the bike turned the corner, their bodies leaned into the motion, moving as one. Physically they were in tune, even if mentally they were still some distance apart. But in that split second, Maggie realized that she had never felt better in her entire life.

The ride to the fairgrounds seemed too short, and she was almost reluctant to get off the bike, to distance herself from Jake, but when he turned his questioning eyes on her, she forced herself to pull off her helmet and get off.

"You enjoyed that, didn't you?" he said, surprise lacing his voice.

Maggie looked away from him. "It's growing on me."

"Maybe we should keep going. Just head out on the open road and go wherever the mood strikes us. We could have a wonderful adventure."

His words conjured up all sorts of ideas in her head. "What a thought," she murmured. "But it's not realistic. We have responsibilities. At least I do."

"Only to yourself. Only to be happy."

"I am happy," she said, wondering why she couldn't put more enthusiasm in her voice. "I'll be even happier if I see a blue ribbon around Henry's neck."

"Just like a woman to put a noose around a guy's neck."

Maggie made a face. "Very funny. Come on."

She led the way across the parking lot, noting the stream of cars beginning to pull in. It was opening day at the fair and families with young children were taking advantage of the early-afternoon admission price.

Just behind the opening gates, she could see the carnival rides and games, and the Ferris wheel looming high over the fairgrounds. Laughter was in the air as well as the smells of childhood: popcorn, hot dogs, pretzels and cotton candy. She felt like a kid again.

"I bet you like the roller coasters, the thrill rides," she said to Jake.

"Of course. What about you?"

"I like to keep my feet on the ground."

Jake pulled out his wallet as they got to the front gate and paid for his ticket while Maggie presented her exhibitor pass, good for one day's admission to the grounds.

"The exhibits are in those barnlike buildings," Maggie said, pointing away from the carnival. "Over by the racetrack."

"Do they put all the zucchinis together?" Jake asked. "Maybe there's a Henrietta in there just perfect for Henry."

Maggie smiled. "Why not? Love seems to be in the air these days. I saw Mr. Pastorini this morning. He is quite taken with your aunt."

"Apparently, the feeling is mutual. I can't imagine what they're thinking, hooking up at their age."

"That's because you don't have any romance in your soul. I think it's cute."

"Cute? They'll mix their money, wind up getting a divorce and everything will be a mess."

"Gee, I hope they don't invite you to the wedding."

"I'll be long gone by then," he replied, digging his hands into the pockets of his jeans.

"Right. I almost forgot." She tilted her head toward the building in front of them. "Henry's in there."

Jake strode forward, but Maggie hesitated, feeling a momentary anxiety about the verdict. When Jake got to the door of the building and she hadn't moved, he walked back over to her, concern etched in the lines of his face.

"What's the problem, Maggie?"

She offered him an uncertain smile. "I'm not sure I want to know."

"This really means a lot to you, doesn't it?"

"Yes. I know it seems silly. A grown woman caring about a zucchini."

"It's not the zucchini, it's what it stands for, right?"

She nodded, feeling both annoyed and relieved that he seemed to understand her so well.

"If the zucchini wins, you win," Jake added.

She hugged her arms around her waist and nodded.

Jake shook his head. "Who you are is not wrapped up in that zucchini. I wish you could see that."

"I do see it," she said. "But I've never been a winner, Jake. I always lose. My brothers won dozens of trophies. They were star athletes, scholars, the most popular kids, no matter where we went. But I wasn't any of those things. They even forgot to take my picture for the yearbook my senior year. I was practically invisible."

Maggie didn't look at Jake when she finished speaking. She didn't want to see amusement on his face or, worse yet, pity. In fact, she had no clue why she had just poured out her heart to him. He didn't care about feelings, about fears and certainly not about fitting in.

Jake didn't say a word for a long moment and then he simply took her in his arms and gave her a hug, pressing her face against his chest. "You're a winner, no matter what happens with Henry. You've got to find your happiness inside. Live your own life. Make your own choices."

"Like you?" she asked, pulling away from him and tilting her head up so she could see his face.

"I know where you're coming from," he admitted. "I spent a lot of my life on a treadmill, never getting anywhere but unable to admit failure and just get off. But I've gotten off now. I'm doing what I want. So should you."

Maggie nodded, taking a deep breath. "I'm doing what I want now, too. Whatever happens with Henry, I'll be okay." A dimple curved in her cheek. "But I'd still like to win."

Maggie led the way into the exhibit hall, her heart quickening as they got close to the vegetable booth. Her gaze shot down the rows, until she saw Henry, a bright red ribbon around his neck.

She hurried over to his spot and ran the edge of the ribbon through her fingers.

"Second place. Not bad. Are you disappointed?" Jake asked.

Maggie looked over at the giant zucchini next to Henry with the blue ribbon. "I can't argue with that."

She glanced down at her watch. "I should probably get back to town. I have to be at work at four."

"That's two hours from now. We're at the fair, honey. Let's have some fun."

"What do you want to do?"

He tilted his head in consideration. "Tunnel of love?"

She rolled her eyes. "Pick something else."

"Okay, let's go see the ponies run."

"Half an hour, Jake, and then we head back. I cannot afford to be late. The last thing I need is another problem with Harry Stone."

Jake flung his arm around her shoulders. "Relax. You're with me. What could go wrong?"

About a million things, Maggie thought, but that didn't stop her from slipping her own arm around his waist. For the next half hour, they were just two people having a good time. She wasn't going to think any further than that.

"Come on, Black Magic. Go! Go! Go!" Maggie screamed as the horses tore down the homestretch.

Jake looked at the excitement on her face and smiled to himself. Watching Maggie was better than any race he could think of.

"Oh, no, here comes the gray," she said worriedly. "Do something, Jake. Yell."

"I don't think he'll hear me."

"Come on, Blackie. Run, baby, run!" she shouted.

The horses came to the finish line dead even, and then Black Magic inched his way across. The winner by a nose.

"He did it. He did it." Maggie flung her arms around Jake and gave him a hug of delight.

He took advantage of the situation and planted a warm, loving kiss on her lips.

Breathlessly she looked up at him, and Jake's arms tightened around her. For a moment, he didn't think he could let her go. She was such a joy to be with, natural, honest, satisfied with the simple things in life like a good-size zucchini and a two-dollar bet.

He lowered his head and kissed her again, wishing she would push him away and hoping to hell that she wouldn't.

She didn't. Her response was as generous as she was, giving him back everything that he wanted, that he needed, everything that he had thought he had lost.

"We better cash my ticket," she said, smiling while she pulled away from his kiss. "This must be my lucky day."

"Mine, too," he replied, smiling back at her.

They were walking away from the track and toward the ticket windows when Jake suddenly stopped, his gaze catching on a very familiar face. With an abrupt move, he yanked Maggie behind a pillar.

"What was that for?" she complained.

"Harry Stone."

"What?"

"He's over there by the window."

"No way. He's supposed to be at work." Maggie leaned her head around the pillar so she could take a closer look. It *was* Harry Stone. He was wearing his usual navy blue suit and black loafers, but he was not alone. His arm was draped around the shoulders of a beautiful young woman. "Oh my goodness," Maggie muttered.

"Who's he with?" Jake asked.

"I don't know, but I don't think it's his wife." Maggie grabbed Jake's arm. "They're coming this way. What are we going to do? If he sees me with you, he's going to fire me."

Jake shifted her around so that her back was to the approaching man. "Just stay still. He seems to be pretty wrapped up with his date right now."

Maggie edged herself against the pillar, praying they would go unnoticed as she heard his voice just off to the side of her.

"I'll get it for you, I promise," Harry said.

"Oh, you're such a sweetie. But I want the sapphire ring. I think it will go with my eyes, don't you?"

"I think your eyes will outshine any ring I could give you." Harry kissed her on the lips, and they walked back out toward the track.

"He's having an affair," Maggie said, shaking her head in wonder. "With a woman young enough to be his daughter."

"Hmm...I think I'm beginning to get the picture," Jake replied.

"I'm not. I can't believe a woman like that would go out with a man like him."

"She doesn't want him. She wants his wallet."

"But he's not rich. He probably makes a good salary, but he has a wife to support or at least pay alimony to."

Jake's eyes narrowed. "Exactly. He must be getting some extra money somewhere. We need to get back to the hotel. Right now."

"Why? What's the rush? I thought you wanted to play."

"I have to check something out and now is a good time, since Mr. Stone is occupied. I'm going to need your help."

"To do what?"

"Get me between the sheets," he said with a wicked smile.

Chapter Eleven

"When you said sheets, I didn't think you meant it literally," Maggie muttered as they walked into the main linen closet for housekeeping at the hotel. "I can't believe I told that outrageous lie to get Maria out of here for a few minutes. You are trouble, Jake Hollister. Big trouble."

"Not as much trouble as Harry Stone," he said, searching through the pile of sheets.

"What exactly are you looking for?"

"New sheets. Harry paid for five hundred new sheets last week. I don't see them."

"I don't think there have been any deliveries of new sheets, Jake."

"And no deliveries of shampoo or soap or chateaubriand for the restaurant."

"I'm not following you."

Jake leaned over and closed the door behind her. "Someone is padding the books," he said. "There are checks being paid out to vendors but no evidence of deliveries.''

"And you think Mr. Stone is responsible?"

"Yes. Seeing him today at the track only confirmed my suspicions."

"What do you do now?"

"Talk to Aunt Ida and see how she wants to handle the situation. We don't want him to run before we find out how much damage he's done."

Maggie shook her head in bemusement. "I can't believe he would do such a thing. Although, maybe that's why he got so mad when I promised the guest in the penthouse suite a complimentary bathrobe, which is standard for that room. He screamed at me and wrote me up for insubordination."

Jake nodded. "Because you were so attentive to the guests, you were putting him in touchy situations. You thought you were offering the standard services, but he was trying to cut corners and pocket some extra cash."

"Maybe it's not him. Maybe it's somebody else. The accountant or the assistant manager."

Jake shook his head. "I don't think so. Nothing goes on in this hotel without Harry being aware of it."

Maggie checked her watch. "I'm due to go on my shift." She reached for the door and turned the knob, but it didn't budge. She tried again, a sinking feeling hitting her deep in her stomach as she looked at Jake in horror. "I can't believe this. We're locked in. You locked us in."

"I just shut the door."

"It locks from the other side. And we sent Maria on a wild-goose chase."

Jake smiled and shrugged. "Guess we'll have to find something to do with all these sheets."

"That's not funny. I have to go to work. If I'm late, he'll fire me."

"He's probably not even back from the track yet, relax. Besides, I'm not going to let anyone fire you for helping me."

Maggie sighed, knowing that railing against a locked door wasn't going to do any more good than screaming at Jake. Instead, she sat down on a pile of blankets and stretched out her legs.

Jake looked at her in surprise. "That's it? That's the extent of your fury? I'm impressed."

"Why, because I'm not hysterical? You don't have a very high opinion of women, do you?" Maggie asked. She patted a pile of blankets next to her. "Why don't you sit down and tell me all about it?"

"There's nothing to tell," he said with a frown. "And I don't hate all women, only certain women."

"Like your ex-wife and probably anyone else who tries to get close to you."

Jake walked over to the door and futilely tried the handle again.

"It's locked, Jake. You have no other alternative but to sit here and talk to me." She paused, waving an arm around their small prison. "Since we're already close, let's get even closer."

"Fine with me," he said, squatting in front of her. He placed his hands on either side of her face and kissed her on the lips, long and slow and so deeply she almost forgot that kissing him was not what she'd had in mind.

"Jake, stop. I want to talk."

"Women always want to talk."

"Think of it as foreplay."

Jake sat back on his heels and shook his head. "I can think of a lot of other things I'd rather do as foreplay."

"Well, this is my choice." Maggie leaned back against the wall while Jake gave up and settled on a pile of blankets opposite her.

"Tell me about your ex-wife," Maggie directed.

Jake's mouth drew into a long, taut line. "Carole was beautiful, ambitious and a debutante. We got married when we were in our early twenties."

"How long have you been divorced?"

"Almost two years."

"What happened?" Maggie prodded. "Unless you really don't want to tell me."

He shrugged. "It's not that big of a deal. Carole and I didn't want the same things out of life. In the beginning, I thought we did. She was the perfect wife for an executive. She gave great parties, wore beautiful clothes, even flirted with reluctant investors."

"What a gem."

"Yeah, and she liked jewelry, too. And clothes and money and houses. I spent years killing myself to build her this incredible dream house in Beverly Hills. It had three stories, seven bedrooms, four bathrooms and a guest house by the pool."

"Sounds wonderful."

"But it wasn't enough. She wanted more. An apartment in New York, a condo on Maui." He shrugged, his eyes darkening with pain. "I just kept going to work, trying to make the best deals, acting like a ruthless bastard to anyone who got in my way. And it was all for nothing."

"Because you got divorced," Maggie finished.

He shook his head. "No, because the house burned down. Nothing was left. No furniture, no paintings, not even a photograph. All we had left was a pile of ashes. When I looked at Carole, when I woke up from the nightmare, I realized there was nothing left there, either. Whatever love we had was gone."

He put his head in his hands, hiding his expression from her, and Maggie felt an overwhelming sense of protectiveness. She slid over onto his pile of blankets and put an arm around his shoulders.

"I'm sorry, Jake. I shouldn't have brought it up."

He looked at her with a somber expression on his face. "It doesn't matter."

"But it does. You're still hurting."

"Not because I have any lingering feelings for Carole or for that god-awful house. I just feel angry that I wasted so much time trying to be somebody I wasn't."

"I know what you mean. Trying to fit into the marine way of life was never easy for me."

"But you're still pretending," he said. "You're no more the happy homemaker than you were the marine daughter."

"Yes, I am," she said defensively. "Okay, I admit my pie needs a little work."

"I'm not talking about the damn pie. I'm talking about you." He cupped her face in his hands. "You're a joyous, loving person. But you're working in a rigid job under a rigid man and you're living all alone in a house, trying to find joy in tending a bunch of vegetables."

"You're a fine one to criticize me," she said hotly, pushing his hands away from her face. "You hide behind some tough-guy biker image when in reality you're a spoiled rich kid with an IQ probably higher than my bank account. You're a brilliant businessman."

"I was." He corrected her with a steel glint in his eyes. "But I'm not anymore."

"Yes, you are. You figured out what was going on in this hotel in less than a week while your aunt has probably been in the dark for months. You've got a wonderful mind to go along with your wonderful body, but you're not using it."

"You think I have a nice body?" he questioned, the tension easing from his face.

"We're not talking about that."

"You're the one who brought it up."

She threw up her hands. "Oh, forget it. You just don't want to see the truth. You're a businessman not an adventurer."

"And you're an adventurer, not a homemaker."

"I'm happy the way I am," she said.

"So am I."

"Fine."

"Fine." He paused. "Are we done talking now?"

"I don't have anything left to say to you," she replied.

"Good. Then enough foreplay." He launched his body on top of hers, throwing her backward on the blankets as his mouth descended on hers.

Maggie pushed her hands against his chest, but one touch of his mouth on hers was enough to put an end to any form of resistance. Her blood was boiling from their confrontation, and the adrenaline pumping through her veins had suddenly turned to passion.

She didn't agree with Jake's assessment of her, but she couldn't deny wanting to taste the wild side of life on his lips, wanting to give in to the desire he aroused in her. She had been playing it safe for a long time. She wanted to let loose, really loose.

Wrapping her arms around his back, she rejoiced in the sensation of his body on hers. When he raised his mouth, she pulled him back, thrusting her tongue into his mouth with an assertiveness that surprised both of them. Jake groaned and kissed her back, his fingers slipping inside her collar, fiddling with the buttons on her shirt until he had freed the top two. And then his palm slid inside her blouse, caressing her breast through the lacy silk of her bra.

"You're driving me crazy," he muttered, kissing the side of her neck and the lobe of her ear. "Don't stop."

"I don't want to." But even as she said the words, Maggie heard a rumbling at the door, voices that slowly slipped into her consciousness. "Oh, God, someone's coming in!"

Jake sat back on his heels while Maggie's hands rushed to her chest, fiddling with the buttons on her blouse. The key slipped into the lock. The knob turned. The door opened, and Maggie jumped to her feet, Jake getting up behind her.

At first, she saw only the maid's amused face, and Maggie ran her fingers through her hair, trying to put it into some semblance of order.

"Don't bother. We're busted," Jake said from behind her.

"We got locked in," Maggie said to Maria, trying to regain her poise, but it quickly slipped away when Maria stepped aside and Harry Stone's glowering image replaced hers. "Mr. Stone," Maggie said, feeling a sense of hopelessness invade her soul.

"Get out, Miss Gordon, and I mean out. Out of the closet. Out of the hotel and out of my life. You're finished."

Maggie looked at him in horror and then back at Jake who put a reassuring hand on her shoulder. Now it would come, the explanations to show that her behavior was not as bad as it seemed, although rolling around in the linen closet was probably a stretch. But the other incidents had been at Jake's and Ida Castleton's instigation. She was blameless.

But Jake wasn't saying anything. His body was tense, and she could sense a repressed anger burning through him, but his mouth remained tightly closed. She didn't understand. Why was he letting her take the heat?

"I think you should consider finding another hotel," Mr. Stone added pointedly to Jake. "We don't tolerate this kind of behavior at the Castleton Hotel."

That should get a rise out of him, Maggie thought. Now, he'd jump into the breach, tear Harry Stone apart, limb by limb or at least word by word. But Jake didn't move and Mr. Stone was walking away.

"Wait," she said frantically. "Mr. Stone, I can explain."

"No, you can't," Jake said quietly. He met her indignant look with a hard, unrelenting gaze. "You can't."

"He's right," Mr. Stone added. "There's nothing to explain. Your behavior has been abominable for weeks and this is simply the last straw. Turn in your uniform and pick up your paycheck on the way out the door."

Maggie fumed silently as he walked away. Maria sent her an apologetic look.

"Sorry, I didn't know you were still in here."

"We accidentally got locked in," Jake explained. "Why don't we get out of here, Maggie?"

"Why don't you get out of here and out of *my* life," Maggie snapped. "You've done enough damage, haven't you?"

"Look, we're going to sort this out."

"When? This is my job we're talking about. I need money to pay my bills, to buy food, to get my house."

"Your house. Don't you think about anything else?"

"No, because it's the only thing I can count on. I know it will be there when I get home. That it won't let me down."

"I'm not letting you down, either. But we have to handle this in just the right way."

"Oh, save it," she said wearily. "I'm done arguing with you. I'm done playing games. Do whatever the heck you want."

"Maggie, wait," Jake said as she walked out of the room. "Everything is going to be all right."

She turned, cutting off the rest of what he was going to say with one fiery look. "It's not going to be all right. It will never be the same. Because you came here and messed everything up. I don't want to like you. I don't want to want you. I don't want to go to bed every night thinking about you, wondering what it would be like between us. I just want you to go. You're the wanderer. Why don't you wander somewhere else and leave me in peace?" Her words ended on a broken sob, and she hastily turned away, running out of the room before Jake could do anything but shake his head in frustration.

He wanted to call her back, to tell her...what? He ran a hand through his hair and sighed. He was moving on. In a couple of days he'd be gone. And his feelings for Maggie would be a pleasant memory. Or would they?

God, he wanted her, more than anyone in his life. He had felt passion for Carole, certainly, but not this deep, burning need that didn't seem to want to go away. And he didn't like it any more than she did, because he was not the man for Maggie. She was staying in one place, and he was moving on. She wanted to play it safe. He wanted adventure. She wanted a house, and he wanted nothing to do with four walls and a mortgage. No more big dreams to be shattered. No more hope to be replaced by despair. He wasn't going to get hurt again.

So, why did his body ache? Why did he feel like the pain in his gut would never go away?

Shaking his head, he walked out of the housekeeping department and down the hall to the elevator. First things first. He had to resolve things with Aunt Ida and give Harry Stone what he deserved. He had felt like a wimp standing there watching Maggie be fired, but if he'd said anything at all, Stone might have run, and that's the last thing he wanted the man to do. He had to find out how deep his thievery had gone so that Ida could hopefully recoup some of her losses.

As he made his way to his aunt's suite, he went over the scenario in his mind. Harry Stone was being sued for divorce. An angry ex-wife probably wanted alimony. He also had a honey on the side, who seemed to like the finer things in life. He was a man being squeezed at both ends, a man who had to find a way to keep everyone happy. So he had fixed the books, paid for shipments that never arrived, probably geting a kickback from the vendors, cut hotel services and in his panic and worry treated the employees like dogs under his whip.

He knocked briskly at Aunt Ida's door just wanting the whole sorry business behind him.

She opened it with a beaming smile. Wearing a colorful silk caftan, she was a picture of joy and happiness, and he sighed again, wishing he didn't have to ruin someone else's day.

"Hello, dear. How are you?"

"Terrible," he said abruptly.

"Oh, my. What's wrong?"

"Stone has been stealing from the hotel. Cooking the books to pay for a mistress and an ex-wife."

Ida's smile faded. "I knew he had problems, but the divorce isn't final yet, at least I don't think it is."

"Maybe not, but Maggie and I just saw him at the track with a sweetie on his arm."

Ida shook her head. "I had no idea. Do you have proof, Jake? I don't want to accuse him unless we're really sure."

He nodded. "I've got proof. You've been paying for lots of things that the hotel never received. All you have to do is check out the linen closets, the kitchen cupboards and the office supplies in the storeroom. He hasn't been particularly subtle."

"I guess I haven't been much of a manager, letting him do all that." Ida walked over to the sofa and sat down, her face suddenly crumpling with the weight of her problems. "The truth is, I don't want to run this hotel, Jake. I haven't wanted to for a long time. That's why I let Harry do what he wanted."

Jake sat down in the chair across from her, disturbed by her unusual seriousness. "Why don't you give it up then? I'm sure the family could put someone else at the helm."

"And have them say I couldn't do it? Are you kidding? Being the only woman out of four brothers, I was always treated like a second-class citizen. I hate to have them think I'm not up to the challenge."

"You're up to the challenge, Aunt Ida. But only if you want to take it on. I know better than anyone what it feels like to be trapped in a life that you don't want."

"It's not that I dislike the hotel, Jake. I'd just like to have a competent manager running things so that I can be free to travel or—be with someone that I care about."

Jake raised an eyebrow. "Are we talking about who I think we're talking about?"

"Antonio is a wonderful man. I know it's only been a couple of days, but sometimes you don't need any more time than that. You know when it's right, because it feels right."

Jake stood up and paced restlessly around the room, her words hitting too close to his own feelings. Maggie felt right. Everything about her felt right, but he didn't want a woman in his life. He wanted to be free to roam, to do whatever he wanted. And what the hell was that, he thought with disgust. He'd already seen most of the country.

"What do you think we should do now?" Ida asked.

Her question dragged his thoughts back to the hotel. "Call the cops, I guess."

"Do you think that will be bad for business?"

"Getting robbed isn't good for business."

"The family dislikes scandal, Jake."

Jake rolled his eyes. "You're not going to let him get away with it, are you? He's a criminal. I don't care how white his collar is. He's still breaking the law."

"I'm going to talk to him first," Ida decided, her submissiveness disappearing as she took charge. "He was a good manager for six years. I want to know what's been happening the last three months. Maybe we can work out a compromise."

"It's your call, but I don't agree. The man has no business managing this hotel. At the very least, he should be terminated." Jake paused, digging his hands into his pockets. "He fired Maggie today."

"Oh, no," Ida said in dismay.

"She's furious because I didn't stick up for her."

"What did she do now?"

Jake cleared his throat. "She was helping me check the linen supply and we got locked in the closet."

Ida burst out laughing. "You and Maggie in the sheets. That's a picture."

"Unfortunately, it was." He paused. "I didn't want to explain because I wanted to talk to you first. Of course, Maggie didn't understand. I felt like a jerk."

"We'll make it up to her. She's been wonderful through all this. Everything will be all right, you'll see."

Jake shook his head. "Not by a long shot, Aunt Ida. I'm leaving just as soon as we resolve Mr. Stone's situation."

"Maybe you should consider staying on indefinitely, taking on Harry's job."

"No, absolutely not."

"Why? You'd be perfect."

"I don't wear suits anymore. And I hate those damn neckties." Jake walked out of the room and shut the door behind him. He was going to leave. He was not going to stay. He was not going to build his life around one woman, one house, or one damn town. Never.

Chapter Twelve

The next day, Maggie was digging in her garden, taking out her frustration on a pile of weeds when the familiar roar of a motorcycle drew her head up.

Jake hurtled into the driveway with a skidding stop and hopped off his bike. He looked good in black jeans and a white shirt. Long, lean and sexy. She scowled at him, and wiped the back of her hand across her sweaty forehead.

"What do you want?"

"Good morning to you, too."

"Just tell me what you want, Jake. I'm busy."

Jake glanced down at his watch. "You better get cleaned up. You're due at work in two hours."

"I don't have a job anymore, remember?"

"It's all been straightened out."

"So quickly?" she asked sarcastically. "I was looking forward to another sleepless night, wondering how I was going to pay the mortgage."

Jake sighed. "I couldn't say anything yesterday. Not until I'd talked to Aunt Ida. Harry could have skipped town."

Maggie shrugged wearily. "Fine. I'm just glad the whole episode is over."

"So am I. I know you were caught in the middle, and I apologize. Aunt Ida should have never told you who I was, never fixed us up together in the first place."

Maggie smiled without any humor. "That was a bust of an idea, wasn't it?"

Jake tipped his head. "I don't know. We had our moments."

Maggie looked down at the weeds and yanked at another root. The last thing she wanted to think about was their moments, especially the last few in the linen closet when she had wanted to make love to him on the floor.

"You're rehired with a clean slate," Jake added. "And no more probation."

Maggie paused, slid off her gloves and slowly got to her feet. Dirt had collected in patches on the knees of her blue jeans, and she reached over to brush it off as she thought about the new situation. "What happened to Mr. Stone?" she asked finally.

"He's going to pay back the money to the hotel and undergo counseling for one year or Aunt Ida will press charges. It turned out old Stoneface just flipped out when his wife ran off with another man. With his ego in shreds, he latched on to the first thing in a short skirt and got himself in a heap of trouble."

"But why take it out on me? I don't understand."

Jake smiled. "Have you ever met Mrs. Stone?"

Maggie shook her head. "No, I've only been at the hotel a few months and I don't recall ever seeing her come in."

"She looks a lot like you. Oh, she's older, but she has the same dark hair and blue eyes. Harry just couldn't stand seeing you at the front desk, not to mention the fact that you kept offering the guests supplies we didn't have."

Maggie thought about what he said and frowned. "I don't know if I can continue to work for Mr. Stone."

"You won't have to. He's going to be transferred to the home office and put in a position where he doesn't control any money. That way we'll be able to make sure he makes enough salary to pay back the hotel."

"That's very generous of the Castletons," Maggie said. "Some companies would have put him in jail."

"That was my first choice," Jake admitted. "But Aunt Ida has the final say. And she has a big heart."

"Yes, she does."

Maggie stared at him for a long moment, wanting to say a lot of things but at the same time wanting to say nothing.

Jake returned her look with one of his own, the muscles in his jaw tightening as if he was also debating what to say. But what could he say—that he loved her—that he wanted to stay in Napa—that he would never leave her? She was realistic enough to know that it wasn't going to happen, no matter how much she wanted it to.

"I guess you'll be leaving now," she said tightly, barely getting the words through her pursed lips.

Jake nodded, slipping his sunglasses back over his eyes. "Yeah, tomorrow. Just going to tie up a few loose ends and hit the road."

"Where are you headed? Another hotel?"

"Not for a while. I'll probably drive up the coast to Mendocino, spend some time on the water."

"Sounds nice."

"Have you been there?"

Maggie smiled grimly. "They don't have a military base there, so no, I haven't seen it."

"Maybe there's still some traveling you need to do."

"I'm happy here."

Jake tipped his head. "Right, we already discussed that point."

Maggie bit down on her lip as another silence enveloped them. The urge to throw herself in his arms and beg him to stay was warring with her need to maintain her pride, her dignity. She didn't want to let him know how much she cared about him, how much she wanted him in her life. It wouldn't accomplish anything. Jake had his life, and she had hers.

"See ya," she said finally, turning her back on him.

He didn't move, and she could feel his gaze boring into her back as she picked up her gardening tools. Finally, she turned to look at him. "Did you want to say something?"

Jake looked back at her for a long heart-stopping moment. "Have a nice life. I don't think I'll ever forget you."

A rush of moisture blurred her vision. "You, too," she muttered and then ran into the house before she lost total control. She shut the front door behind her and leaned against it. She wanted to hear the roar of his engine so that she would know he was gone. But she also wanted to hear his footsteps on the porch, hopelessly wishing one last time that he'd stay.

Her tension increased with every second and then she heard it, the engine, the motorcycle. Jake was gone. And she was alone.

It was okay, she told herself determinedly. She had her job back and her house and a red ribbon from the county fair. She had accomplished everything but the pie, and there was still next year for that. She should be ecstatic, but the empty feeling in her stomach robbed her of joy.

Maybe she was hungry. Maybe an ice-cream cone would do the trick. Yeah, right.

One week later as Maggie finished up her work at the hotel, she knew that nothing was going to do the trick. She missed Jake something fierce. Nothing in her life had prepared her for such depth of emotion. She thought about him every night when she went to bed and every morning when she got up. Every time she saw a motorcycle, she expected to see his sexy grin, his light green eyes, his tight blue jeans. But it was never him. It was always someone else.

She tried everything. Gallons of ice cream. A half-dozen attempts at making the perfect apple pie. She had cleaned every closet in the house and even painted her bedroom. Nothing worked. Her house seemed like an empty shell and at night she wrapped her arms around a feather pillow and wished for something more.

Her breakup with her fiancé had never been this intense. She had felt relief then, not a deep anguish that penetrated her soul. And she had known Jake only a little over a week, such little time to form such a deep attachment, but it had happened. And she didn't know what to do.

"Going home?" Karen asked as Maggie reached inside the drawer for her purse.

Maggie nodded. "Yes, it's been a long week."

"But a pleasant one without Mr. Stone on our backs. I wonder if they're going to promote Connie," she said, referring to the assistant manager.

"I don't think she has that much experience, but maybe Mrs. Castleton will take a chance on her."

"I still can't believe Jake Hollister was really an undercover guest. He sure had me fooled."

Maggie smiled. "I wish I could have told you. Maybe then, everyone would have stopped gossiping about us."

Karen sent her a thoughtful look. "I know you were helping him, but what exactly were you doing in the linen closet?"

"Counting sheets."

Karen laughed. "That's a good one. I would have loved to count sheets with a guy like that. I wonder if he'll ever come back."

Maggie felt a shaft of pain at her friend's simple words. "I doubt it," she said harshly. "He's a wanderer at heart. Doesn't stay too long anywhere."

"Too bad. For a while there, I thought you'd found Mr. Right."

Maggie looked at her in surprise. "Me and a biker? Why would you think that?"

"Oh, because he wasn't really a biker. I know he dressed the part, but he was too courteous, too well educated to really fit that image. And I think you looked kind of cute on the back of his bike."

"It was fun," Maggie admitted. "While it lasted. But now it's over. Good night."

"Good night," Karen replied. "Sleep well."

He was never going to sleep again, Jake decided. It had been three weeks since he'd left the Castleton Hotel, and he hadn't had a good night's rest yet. Mainly because he couldn't get her damn face out of his mind.

Kicking his feet up on the coffee table, he popped open a beer and looked around at his apartment. He hadn't been home in weeks, and there was a fine layer of dust over everything that he owned, which wasn't much. The walls were blank, no pictures, no mementos. His stereo sat on a pile of bricks and boards, and his records were stashed in a milk crate. Some home. His mother would have a heart attack if she saw the place.

His mother. She had ruled him with an iron hand, instructing him on the finer points of life until he knew the rules of etiquette as well as his own name. Where she had left off, Carole had taken over, fine-tuning him to be the perfect man that they both wanted.

And then he had walked out. The fire that destroyed their dream home had also destroyed what was left of their marriage. The thought of rebuilding, of going through the grind all over again had sent him running for the hills. He would not be tied down again. From then on, the rules were his to make or break as he saw fit.

He had been relatively happy the last two years. He had seen most of the United States and quite a few countries in Europe. He had lived like a bum and rejoiced in being dirty and unshaven. He had tried everything from surfing to bungee jumping and he had survived. For what?

The question kept hitting him like a pile of bricks falling on his hard, stubborn head.

For what?

The constant traveling had taken its toll. Although he had spent the last two weeks cruising down the coast of California, he had found the scenery strangely bland without Maggie to share it with, without her crazy sense of humor, her zest for the little things in life.

He shook his head and smiled to himself as he took a long draft of beer. He wondered if she was still poisoning people with her pie, if she had eaten Henry, if she was lonely without him.

The thought came unbidden, and once there, it wouldn't go away. He missed her like crazy. She was the first person he'd met who didn't care if he had money or even a decent haircut.

Why hadn't she asked him to stay?

Because she was too damn stubborn, he realized. Because she wouldn't ask him to stay any more than he would ask her to leave. It had to be his choice. It had to be hers.

A knock came at his door and his heart leaped into his throat. He jumped up off the couch and practically ran to the door, wondering, hoping . . . but his momentary excitement faded as he saw the plump round face of his landlady.

"Hello, Mrs. Riley," he said.

She looked at his two-day-old clothes and beard and frowned. "I wasn't sure if you were back, but I saw the bike."

"Just pulled in a few minutes ago."

"I'm running down to the bank and wondered if you had the rent money."

Jake nodded and pulled out a wad of cash. "I was going to slip it under your door tonight."

Mrs. Riley took it and smiled. "It seems sort of silly your paying rent when you're hardly ever here. But I won't complain."

It was silly, Jake thought. And just about everything else in his life was silly, too. He was thirty-five years old and acting like an irresponsible kid, and he wasn't even enjoying it. That startling revelation hit him hard. He wasn't having a good time anymore. He was just going through the motions.

"Did you want to prepay for next month, too?" Mrs. Riley added. "I know sometimes you take off and don't know when you'll be back."

Jake stared at her for a long moment and suddenly her question became very important.

"I asked you a question, Maggie," Ida Castleton said, tapping her knuckles on the counter. "Did you make your final payment to Antonio? Is the house really yours?"

Maggie stared at the older woman, struck again by her resemblance to Jake, the strong jawline, the twinkling eyes. So caught up was she in the memory that it took a few seconds for the question to sink in. Finally, she nodded. "I'm going to stop by Mr. Pastorini's as soon as I get off work."

"How wonderful. You've worked hard for this."

"Yes, I have," Maggie acknowledged, wishing she could drum up a little more enthusiasm. "Of course, I still have to make the monthly payments to the bank, but I'll have the deed in my name." She paused, noting the other woman's fine linen suit. "You look lovely today. Any special plans?"

Ida blushed. "Actually, Antonio and I are going up to Lake Tahoe this weekend."

"Really?" Maggie asked with a twinkle in her eye. "To gamble?"

"Among other things."

Ida's mysterious answer made Maggie instantly suspicious.

"You're not planning on visiting any of those quaint little chapels up there, are you?"

"Shh, someone will hear you," Ida said quietly, joy bursting out of her eyes. "I'm so happy, Maggie. I never thought I'd be this happy again. You go through life thinking that you're just going to play out the cards you have and then someone suddenly throws in a new one. The game changes and you're a new player."

Maggie nodded, knowing exactly what she meant. "But sometimes the new game isn't any better than the old one."

"You're right, but I'm willing to take the risk. What have I got to lose? I already know what I have right now. What I don't know is what's out there, waiting for me," she said, waving her arm in emphasis. "I have to find out." She paused. "Oh, look, there's Antonio. If you have your check now, you can give it to him and save yourself a trip to his place."

"Right." Maggie reached automatically for her purse and pulled out the check. But she couldn't give it to Mr. Pastorini because he was holding Ida in his arms and kissing her with all the passion of his Italian heritage.

Maggie simply stared, envious of their love, and even more aware of her loneliness. She and Jake had kissed like that. She and Jake had shared moments when they had been completely in tune, laughing at the same thought, frowning at the same problem, kissing with the same need. Kindred spirits. And she had let it all go for a house. Not a home, but a house.

"Well, let's have it," Antonio said, sticking out his hand. "You're probably itching to see your name on that deed."

Maggie stared at him blankly.

"Maggie," Ida said gently. "Are you okay?"

"What's wrong with her?" Antonio asked in a loud whisper. "She looks like she's in a trance."

"She's just thinking," Ida replied. "Probably about her house."

Maggie shook her head as their speculation continued. And then she started to smile, to feel again, to know what she wanted. "Not about the house. About everything else." She shoved the check across the counter. "Here's what I owe you."

"Good. We can walk across the street and get the sale notarized before Ida and I leave for Tahoe."

"No. I can't wait for that. I have to go." She looked at Ida. "I don't know when I'll be back."

"What do you mean?" Ida asked in surprise.

"There's a new trainee starting tomorrow so you shouldn't be shorthanded. I'm sorry if I'm leaving you in the lurch, but there's a whole world out there that I haven't seen yet." Maggie lifted the partition and walked out from behind the desk, unbuttoning the top two buttons on her shirt and pulling at the crisp tie around her neck as she headed for the front door.

"That girl's gone crazy," Antonio proclaimed.

Ida smiled. "She's not crazy. She's in love. Now, if only my nephew would come to his senses."

The adrenaline pumped through Jake's body as he turned off the freeway at the Napa exit and took the highway leading into town. The sky was suddenly bluer. The grass greener. The air sweeter. He was in Maggie country, and he couldn't wait to get even closer, to hold her in his arms, to hear her say his name in passion, in desire.

His whole body tightened at the thought and he pushed the motorcycle to the edge of the speed limit. There was no time to waste. He'd already let weeks go by. Maybe she'd forgotten about him. Maybe she had already set up house with some nine-to-five type in a bad suit.

The thought made him smile. With the kind of trouble she got into, a relationship like that wouldn't last five seconds. She needed someone who could roll with the punches, accept the twists of fate that always intruded on her life, stand by her in the hard times and rejoice in the good times. She needed him. And Lord, he needed her.

He was soaring so fast down the highway that he almost missed her, almost didn't see the orange Volkswagen at the side of the road, the flat tire lying on the ground and the woman wielding the jack like a warrior attacking a beast.

He spun the bike around, making a quick U-turn, and pulled up behind her.

Maggie jumped back at his approach, dropping the jack on the ground with a clutter, one hand flying to her breast. He got off the bike and pulled off his sunglasses. He wanted to see her face, every expression that crossed through her eyes, and he wanted her to see his.

"Need some help?" he asked.

Maggie blinked two times as if she couldn't believe he was standing in front of her. "You. What are you doing here?"

Jake hesitated, uncertainty suddenly hitting him hard. What if she had forgotten about him? What if she didn't want him in her life?

"What are you doing here?" he asked, turning the question around. He looked past her to the pile of clothes stacked in the car. "Going on a trip?"

Maggie drew in a breath. "I'm going to L.A."

"Why?"

"To see someone."

"Who?"

"You."

Jake let out the breath he was holding. "But I'm here."

"Why are you here?" she asked with the same intensity.

"I came to see you."

Maggie grinned and the sun came back into his life. "I want to be with you, Jake. I don't care where you live or where I live. The house doesn't matter anymore. Just let me ride with you on your bike for a while, as long as you want. I won't tie you down, I promise."

"Really?" He looked at her in amazement. "You'd give up your house for me?"

She shrugged. "It's just a house, not a home. I realize that now. My mother knew it all along. That's why she didn't mind the traveling, because she loved my dad. But I couldn't do it with Mark because I didn't love him."

"Does this mean I can join the marines?"

"Not on your life."

Jake laughed and drew her into his arms. "I've been doing some thinking, too. I want to be tied down, as long as the strings lead to you. I blamed all my problems on a house, Maggie, a stupid house. But it wasn't the problem. My marriage was the problem."

"I understand, Jake." She put a finger up to his lips and traced the curve of his mouth.

He nodded. "I know you do. That's why I came back. You brought me to life, Maggie. Now, I want to share yours, if you'll let me."

"Are you sure? I can't cook."

"I'll cook for both of us. I don't care about those things. I don't want you to pretend with me, not ever."

"Oh, Jake." Maggie wrapped her arms around his waist and buried her face against his chest, relishing the warmth and pleasure of his embrace. It had never felt as sweet as it did now. "I don't care what we do or where we live, let's just do it together."

"My thoughts exactly."

Jake tilted her head up with his hand and stared down into her eyes for a long, intense, cherished moment. Then he lowered his head and kissed her on the mouth, loving, generous, the way she knew he would always be with her.

"There's something else you should know," Jake added, lifting his head to smile down at her. "I'm going to start wearing a suit."

"Oh, no," she said in mock horror. "Why would you want to do that?"

"Because I'm thinking about taking a job." He cleared his throat. "The truth is, you were right about my getting bored with my life-style. Troubleshooting at the hotels has only made me want to get back into business, at least part of it. I don't ever want to kill myself for a buck again, but I do like the challenge of making something work."

"Good. Because I just quit my job, and we're going to need some money to live on."

"You quit?"

She nodded. "I figured I wouldn't be back this way for a while. At least, I hoped when I found you that you would want me to stay."

"Are you kidding? I don't ever want you to leave. But I think I can get your job back." He grinned at her. "Aunt Ida has asked me to be the new manager at the hotel. Seems she wants to spend more time with her new husband, Antonio."

Maggie's eyes opened wide and then she burst out laughing. "I get to work for you?"

"*With* me, honey. Right alongside. We make a pretty good team, don't you think?"

"But I attract trouble. Strange men walk off the street and kiss me."

"Not while I'm around," he growled, putting his own sealing kiss on her lips. "And I'm going to change your job description, give you more flexibility, more room to do what you do best, which is make people happy."

"That sounds great. I do love working at the hotel." She shook her head in sudden amusement. "But we have to take a trip first. My brother is getting married this weekend in Texas, and I want you to go with me. I want you to meet my family, and I want them to meet you. No more pretenses, Jake. You're you and I'm me, and they can damn well accept us for who we are. Right?"

"Right. But don't get too far away. I may your need self-defense skills when I meet your father."

She smiled. "Don't worry, I'll protect you—on one condition."

He raised an eyebrow. "What?"

"You tell me the secret to your apple pie."

Jake grinned. "Some things are sacred."

"Jake."

"Okay. Okay. It's in the sugar and lemon juice ratio. Your recipe had it backward."

"But I changed the measurement dozens of times."

"Yes, but you were too conservative, unwilling to be bold, to take a chance." Jake touched her lips with one finger. "You take a pinch of sweet—" he touched his own lips "—and a pinch of sour, and together you have the perfect combination." He kissed her on the lips to seal his point.

Maggie chuckled as he lifted his head. "You might have to show me again."

"Any time you want. But right now I think we should celebrate."

Maggie looked into his sparkling green eyes and their gazes locked on the same thought. "Ice cream," she said.

"Afternoon Delight," Jake replied with a wicked grin.

"Definitely."

Maggie stood on her tiptoes and kissed his lips, his cheek and the side of his neck, oblivious to the cars going by. She was in love, and she didn't care if the whole world knew it.

"Maggie, I was talking about ice cream," Jake said gruffly.

She smiled up at him. "I have a better idea. And believe me, your afternoon will definitely be a delight."

* * * * *

Silhouette
ROMANCE™

COMING NEXT MONTH

#1000 REGAN'S PRIDE—Diana Palmer
Celebration 1000!
Rancher Ted Regan was falling for the very beautiful—and impossibly young—Coreen Tarleton. But how could he take her into his heart when their past weighed so heavily on his mind?

#1001 MARRY ME AGAIN—Suzanne Carey
Celebration 1000!
Strange dreams told Enzo Rossi of another life where he had loved—and lost—centuries ago. Now the bride who haunted his nights had become a reality. Did he dare love Laura Rossi again?

#1002 A FATHER'S PROMISE—Helen R. Myers
Celebration 1000!—Fabulous Fathers
John Paladin had once run from Dana Dixon—into the arms of another woman. Now the rugged rancher was home with his infant son—and a slim hope that he'd win Dana back.

#1003 THE BACHELOR CURE—Pepper Adams
Celebration 1000!
Molly Fox returned to her hometown just as handsome Clay Cusak was planning on leaving. Could the lovely doctor prescribe some permanent medicine for Clay's wandering heart?

#1004 ROMANCING CODY—Rena McKay
Celebration 1000!
As a girl, it hurt Trisha Lassiter to learn that Cody Malone only wanted her for one thing—her brains. Now she was a woman and Cody still wanted her—*all* of her....

#1005 CHILD OF HER DREAMS—Sandra Steffen
Celebration 1000!—Spellbound
Though Lexa Franklin had forgotten her past, she'd gained a talent that could help Cade Sullivan find his lost child. But loving the handsome father made her search more urgent—and more dangerous!

Take 4 bestselling love stories FREE

Plus get a FREE surprise gift!

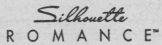

SILHOUETTE... Where Passion Lives

Don't miss these Silhouette favorites by some of our most
distinguished authors! And now you can receive a discount by
ordering two or more titles!

SD	#05772	FOUND FATHER by Justine Davis	$2.89	☐
SD	#05783	DEVIL OR ANGEL by Audra Adams	$2.89	☐
SD	#05786	QUICKSAND by Jennifer Greene	$2.89	☐
SD	#05796	CAMERON by Beverly Barton	$2.99	☐
IM	#07481	FIREBRAND by Paula Detmer Riggs	$3.39	☐
IM	#07502	CLOUD MAN by Barbara Faith	$3.50	☐
IM	#07505	HELL ON WHEELS by Naomi Horton	$3.50	☐
IM	#07512	SWEET ANNIE'S PASS by Marilyn Pappano	$3.50	☐
SE	#09791	THE CAT THAT LIVED ON PARK AVENUE by Tracy Sinclair	$3.39	☐
SE	#09793	FULL OF GRACE by Ginna Ferris	$3.39	☐
SE	#09822	WHEN SOMEBODY WANTS by Trisha Alexander	$3.50	☐
SE	#09841	ON HER OWN by Pat Warren	$3.50	☐
SR	#08866	PALACE CITY PRINCE by Arlene James	$2.69	☐
SR	#08916	UNCLE DADDY by Kasey Michaels	$2.69	☐
SR	#08948	MORE THAN YOU KNOW by Phyllis Halldorson	$2.75	☐
SR	#08954	HERO IN DISGUISE by Stella Bagwell	$2.75	☐
SS	#27006	NIGHT MIST by Helen R. Myers	$3.50	☐
SS	#27010	IMMINENT THUNDER by Rachel Lee	$3.50	☐
SS	#27015	FOOTSTEPS IN THE NIGHT by Lee Karr	$3.50	☐
SS	#27020	DREAM A DEADLY DREAM by Allie Harrison	$3.50	☐

(limited quantities available on certain titles)

AMOUNT	$	
DEDUCT: **10% DISCOUNT FOR 2+ BOOKS**	$	
POSTAGE & HANDLING	$	_____
($1.00 for one book, 50¢ for each additional)		
APPLICABLE TAXES*	$	_____
TOTAL PAYABLE	$	_____
(check or money order—please do not send cash)		

To order, complete this form and send it, along with a check or money order
for the total above, payable to Silhouette Books, to: **In the U.S.:** 3010 Walden
Avenue, P.O. Box 9077, Buffalo, NY 14269-9077; **In Canada:** P.O. Box 636,
Fort Erie, Ontario, L2A 5X3.

Name: _____

Address: _____ City: _____

State/Prov.: _____ Zip/Postal Code: _____

*New York residents remit applicable sales taxes.
Canadian residents remit applicable GST and provincial taxes.   SBACK-JM

V Silhouette®

Silhouette

SPECIAL EDITION™

That SPECIAL Woman!

MYSTERY WIFE
Annette Broadrick

She awoke in a French hospital—and found handsome Raoul DuBois, claiming she was his wife, Sherye, mother of their two children. But she didn't recognize him or remember her identity. Whoever she was, Sherye grew more attached to the children every day—and the growing passion between her and Raoul was like nothing they'd ever known before....

She's friend, wife, mother—she's you! And beside each Special Woman stands a wonderfully *special* man. It's a celebration of our heroines—and the men who become part of their lives.

Don't miss THAT SPECIAL WOMAN! each month—from some of your special authors! Only from Silhouette Special Edition!

TSW494

As seen on TV!
Free Gift Offer

With a Free Gift proof-of-purchase from any Silhouette® book,
you can receive a beautiful cubic zirconia pendant.

This gorgeous marquise-shaped stone is a genuine cubic
zirconia—accented by an 18" gold tone necklace.

(Approximate retail value $19.95)

Send for yours today...
compliments of 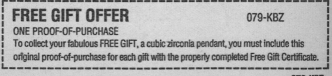 *Silhouette*®

To receive your free gift, a cubic zirconia pendant, send us one original proof-of-purchase, photocopies not accepted, from the back of any Silhouette Romance™, Silhouette Desire®, Silhouette Special Edition®, Silhouette Intimate Moments® or Silhouette Shadows™ title for January, February or March 1994 at your favorite retail outlet, together with the Free Gift Certificate, plus a check or money order for $2.50 (do not send cash) to cover postage and handling, payable to Silhouette Free Gift Offer. We will send you the specified gift. Allow 6 to 8 weeks for delivery. Offer good until March 31st, 1994 or while quantities last. Offer valid in the U.S. and Canada only.

Free Gift Certificate

Name: _____

Address: _____

City: _____ State/Province: _____ Zip/Postal Code: _____

Mail this certificate, one proof-of-purchase and a check or money order for postage and handling to: SILHOUETTE FREE GIFT OFFER 1994. In the U.S.: 3010 Walden Avenue, P.O. Box 9057, Buffalo NY 14269-9057. In Canada: P.O. Box 622, Fort Erie, Ontario L2Z 5X3

FREE GIFT OFFER   079-KBZ
ONE PROOF-OF-PURCHASE
To collect your fabulous FREE GIFT, a cubic zirconia pendant, you must include this original proof-of-purchase for each gift with the properly completed Free Gift Certificate.

079-KBZ